I0582547

BRANDED IN LOVE

USA TODAY BESTSELLING AUTHOR
SILVANA G. SÁNCHEZ

Copyright © 2023 by Silvana G. Sánchez. All rights reserved.

No part of this book may be reproduced in any form or by any electronic or mechanical means, including information storage and retrieval systems, without written permission from the author, except for the use of brief quotations in a book review.

This is a work of fiction. Names, characters, places, and incidents either are product of the author's imagination or are used fictitiously. Any resemblance to actual persons, living or dead (or undead), events, or locales is entirely coincidental.

Cover design by *SP Designs*.

Edited by Julie Cocaigne.

BRANDED IN LOVE

BAD BOY SHIFTERS OF THE
UNNATURAL BRETHREN

Branded in Love

Runt of the Pack

Embers of Fate

*Be the first to know when Silvana's next book is available!
Follow her on Bookbub to get an alert whenever she has a
new release, preorder, or discount!*

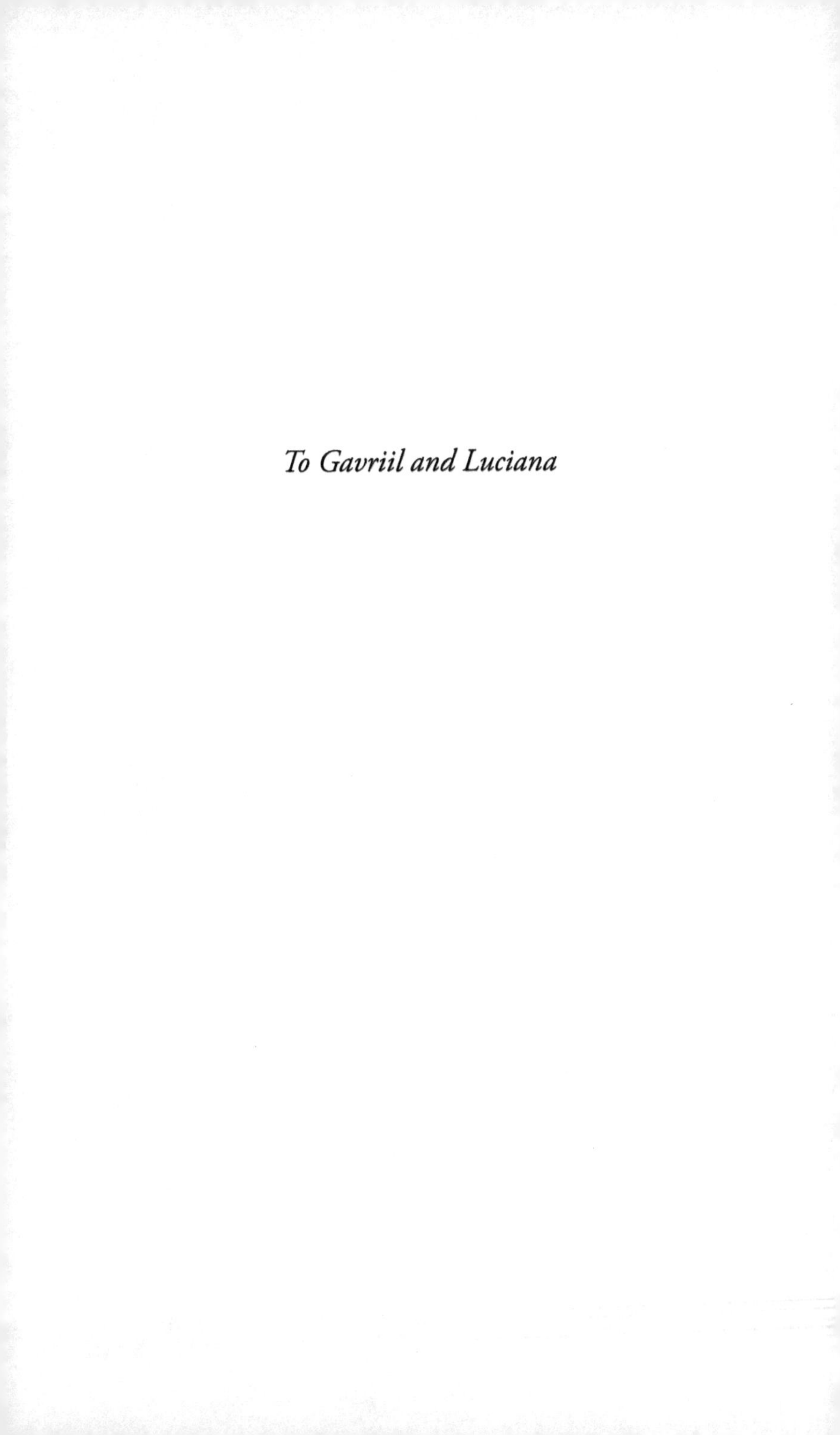

To Gavriil and Luciana

I love you as certain dark things are to be loved,
in secret, between the shadow and the soul.

— PABLO NERUDA

A NOTE FROM THE AUTHOR

The events that take place in this story occurred immediately after the ones related in *Call of Blood*, five years before those narrated in *Cast in Blood.*

As you dive into these pages, dearest reader, I ask of you one thing: do not be influenced by Gavriil's former character. In this book, you will meet Gavriil Alexeev as he was, the man and shifter warlock the Ursa King used to be.

With each page turned, it's my sincere wish that the layers that cloak the Ursa King may be shed, and hopefully, you will see him in a new light as it becomes clear that even the vilest villain has a heart—and an origin story.

If this is your first acquaintance with the characters in this series, I wish you enjoy Luciana and

Gavriil's love story. And if you're tempted by this glimpse of their world, you might want to read the Unnatural Brethren series afterward.

Until then…

In love and gratitude,

Silvana.

Good kings make the rules. Great kings rise above them.

The King of the Ursa Clan never takes a holiday. But for the first time in almost a decade, Gavriil Alexeev allows himself some respite.

The powerful warlock bear shifter flees from the tragedies that haunt him and seeks refuge in Rome. Little does he know he'll come across his fated mate.

She's not a shifter, nor a witch. And as the king, his clan will take no other match, especially not one that unleashes an unprecedented feud between vampires and bear shifters.

Good things come to those who wait. Great things come to those who chase them.

Luciana Marino is ready to pack her heart along with the many antiques she sells in her shop near the Villa Borghese. Not even hunky runway model, Trent, has been able to make her fall head over heels.

But when Gavriil Alexeev enters the picture, all of her certainties are shaken. And before Luciana realizes it, magic, danger, and true love wrap her in an unstoppable whirlwind.

It comes to me from time to time. The blur of violence.

The growls.

The bites.

The blood.

Bella's screams.

It happens in a daze. When I come back to myself and the bear is tucked away, I see Grisha, rabid from the fight. Blackened eyes with an empty stare. Claws ready to rip apart anyone who dares cross his path.

"Bella…" I breathe as the blood in my veins freezes. "RUN!"

PRESENT DAY

Rome, Italy.

Gavriil
Alexeev

1

GAVRIIL

un, Gavriil.

One last sprint, I tell myself. *Push yourself harder until you're so exhausted that your mind will have no choice but to shut down.* There's no escaping the images that have haunted me for the past two years, I know that. But running puts those thoughts to sleep, however briefly. Sasha does not agree. He practically forced me into taking this getaway.

The Villa Borghese is quiet this late in the afternoon. Almost closing time. It's difficult to regret leaving my lair in Saint Petersburg when the Roman air is so warm, the skies are pristine blue, and I'm surrounded by leafy woods. Especially when the

7

harshest winter strikes back home. I'm lucky to keep a house in the Eternal City.

It dawns on me then. This is the first holiday I've ever taken since becoming the leader of the Ursa Clan.

I make one last sprint, fired up as the adrenaline pumps hard through my veins. My pulse throbs in my chest and limbs. My breathing quickens. Beads of sweat break from my skin and slowly drip down my back and chest. The sole thing that can compare to this delight is spending the weekend at my dacha by the riverside, throwing spears and axes.

The dirt road lies ahead. Trees seem to lean over me as I glimpse the park's exit. It's a short walk from there to the house... Sasha must be out of his mind right now. I left without giving him so much as a warning. We just arrived in Rome this morning. However, he could track me in a heartbeat if he really needed to. He's giving me the space I need to clear my mind.

Daylight wanes. The streetlights flash in the distance. The shops begin to close. I almost reach the gates when I pick up an extraordinary scent, feminine, compelling, and sweet. The minute it reaches my lungs, the bear in me reacts, demanding that I track her.

I slow my pace until I stop. *This can't be happening. I don't need this right now.* But my bear won't listen. It's unrelenting whenever he storms through. I stare at the open gates. Chest heaving with exhaustion, I look back.

My jaw clenches. A low growl lingers in my chest. "Fuck it," I mutter.

Succumbing to my bear's demands, I rush back on the road, tracing this maddening scent. And the closer I get, the more it drills into my core, pushing me further.

Then suddenly, it changes.

I stop short, confused. "What the…?" My gaze narrows, sweeping the park with a glance in all directions. Little by little, my expression shifts from bemusement into undiluted fierceness. There's another scent in the park, hovering over the first. So much so, it completely overpowers it.

Only one creature can absorb someone's essence with such viciousness. A monster that feeds off the energy of others. It is ruthless, selfish, and its hunger knows no satisfaction.

I clench my jaw. "Fucking vampire…"

Now the search turns into a hunt. I dart through the trees, away from the road, and into the woods.

2

LUCIANA

I'm going through the last box. I can't help but sigh as I hold my grandfather's gorgeous bracket clock. My grandmother's art déco rings and pendants are there too... It took me months to decide to part with them, and now that I have these treasures in the shop, I'm not sure I want to sell them. But a girl's gotta eat.

"Are you ready, *cara?*" Marco peeps into the storage room. "It's closing time."

"Yeah, I'm just sorting these out." I return the clock to the box and watch it with an empty stare.

Marco steps into the room and crouches beside me. His hand smooths over my back. "I know it's hard, sweetie. But it's the right thing to do."

My lips stretch into a bitter smile. "I know..."

He holds me gently, and we both get on our feet. "Do you want to watch a movie tonight? Or maybe you have plans already?" he asks.

"Plans?" I wince. "Do you know who I am?" I tease as I grab my bag and turn off the lights.

"You know, I just don't get it." Marco scrunches his nose. "We're both impossibly gorgeous. And yet, we're still single." He shakes his head, then grabs his car keys off the desk. "I mean, how can that be, Luciana?" Now he crosses his arms over his chest and stares at me dead in the eye. "*Please* explain."

My eyes fly open. "Wow. That's a loaded question!" I snigger. "Let me think about this." I pause for effect. "We haven't met the right man, Marco. It's as simple as that... Or maybe there isn't that perfect someone for us. Maybe it's all a stupid fantasy."

He sucks at his teeth, not at all satisfied by my answer. "When I lived in the US, I had no problem meeting hot guys. But here, it's like I'm a ghost —*fantasma!*" He gestures with his hands, then turns to open the glass doors when his gaze suddenly locks on something outside.

"There's that guy again..." he mumbles in Italian.

"What guy?" I slip my bag's leather strap over my shoulder and move closer.

Marco swings his head back, striking green eyes

fixed on mine. "The hot one you've been seeing," he adds, shooting up a groomed eyebrow. "Don't think I haven't noticed."

My cheeks burn. "Nothing escapes you, does it?" I roll my eyes back. "We went out on one date. Anyway, it's nothing serious." I dismiss, shrugging my shoulders.

"Good thing it isn't," he mumbles, looking through the shop's window.

"Oh?" I step closer, intrigued. "Why is that?"

Marco's eyes narrow, sweeping Trent with an appraising stare. "He's handsome as hell, *cara*. But there's something about him... I don't know." He bites the inside of his cheek. "He gives off bad vibes."

I gasp. "You're so superstitious, Marco." Trent calls me outside with a tilt of his head. "Don't tell me you're jealous."

Marco scoffs. "*Geloso, io?*" He scowls. "Excuse me, but there's only one Marco Pellegrini in your life, Luciana. I've known you forever. So, no. That's not it!" Vexed, he pulls the door open. "Hey, *hot dude!*" he calls out. "Yeah, you. You can come in now... I'm leaving."

My eyes are all but bulging. I'm sure I'm blushing. "Goddammit, Marco..." I mutter.

At once, Marco marches down the sidewalk.

When Trent holds the door, I see a handsome man. He's definitely pleasing to the eye, but I feel absolutely nothing. There's no thrill, no stomach dropping to the floor. I could well be flipping the pages of a magazine and see him there.

"*Ciao*, Trent…" I tell him.

"Hey, Luciana." Trent flashes me a smile. I'm sure it's part of his modeling portfolio. He combs back his golden hair with his fingers. This guy is beautiful, and he knows it. I wish I felt something for him, but other than admiring his good looks, there's nothing. Zilch. Nada. "I wanted to stop by, see how you're doing."

"I'm… good." At this point, I'm realizing we haven't moved from the doorway. Should I ask him in? I really want to go home.

Trent exhales a long breath. He's leaning on the door now, scratching his eyebrow. I sense him rattled. Maybe I'm imagining things. I've been working all day. God, I'm so tired.

"Say, uh…" Another enticing smile. For the life of me, I can't understand why he would have an interest in me. He's way out of my league. "I'll walk you home."

"Okay," I tell him. It's just a twenty-minute walk across the park. If he thinks I'm asking him up, he'll be sorely disappointed. I'm not interested in a one-nighter.

I step outside and lock the door. When I turn, I meet his striking blue eyes. His widened pupils swallow me whole. It's a bit unnerving, so I look away fast. We cross the street and walk into the Villa Borghese.

"So, uh…" Trent begins, "I'm thinking about tonight."

"Oh?" I say. "What about tonight?" Here we go. The minute I say no, he'll go away. And you know what? Good riddance. Maybe I'm lonely, but I'm not *that* lonely.

Branches break to my right. I spot movement in the undergrowth. Is that… growling?

"Oh my God!"

3

GAVRIIL

*I*t's almost impossible to focus when the woman's scent overpowers my senses. But the minute my gaze locks on the filthy blood drinker, every primal instinct in me awakens. Not only is he a vampire, my natural enemy, but the demon also pretends to steal the human from me. That alone doubles my wrath against the blood devil.

Every inch of me targets the miserable vampire. I don't think. I let my inner bear take command. And in a flash, I leap out of the woods, grab him by the jacket's lapels, and tackle him to the ground. Immediately, we struggle. I gave him but a split second to sense my presence, but he did.

"Oh my God!" the woman screams, bolting back. "Trent!"

We roll on the dirt until finally, I'm on top of the vampire. In one quick move, I shove my forearm hard against his throat, ready to crush his windpipe. That might give me the leverage I need to rip his head off. "You're not getting away from me," I say through gritted teeth. My beef with vampires goes back a long way, to the one who killed my father. I'll gladly take down a blood drinker anytime. The fact that he's after the woman only strengthens my resolve.

"Get off him!" the woman roars.

I start. *What the…?* Out of the corner of my eye, I see her pick up something from the ground. Is that a… rock? I can't tell. Looking away from the vampire might cost me my life.

"Get off me, Ursa beast!" the vampire all but hisses, squirming under my grip. He must be a young blood demon, otherwise, his strength would have matched mine at the very least. This is almost too easy.

I can't help but smile when he recognizes my true nature. "Not much of a fighter, are you?" I tell him in a hoarse voice, pressing harder.

"I said…" she growls, livid. It's almost as if *she* were the bear shifter. Not me. "Get. Off. Him!"

My brow furrows. I can't turn now. A sudden

blow strikes me hard between my shoulder blades. "OW!" I snarl, grimacing. The hit hurts, but it doesn't feel like a rock. Furious, my head swings towards the woman. Then I see her weapon. Not a rock, but a bag. Ten times heavier than any boulder.

The vampire takes the chance and slithers away from my hold. I get on my feet fast, with sharpened senses, ready to confront the creature's attack. But first... "What do you think you're doing?" I tell her, wincing while I rub my sore neck. "I'm saving your life!"

Her brow furrows, bemused.

"He's a fucking vampire!" I say. I do not need this right now. If her scent weren't driving me mad, I would not even be here.

The woman's lips part. She takes a step back, gripping her bag tight. "A vampire? Are you crazy?" she says, as flabbergasted as I am.

She keeps speaking, but I no longer listen. "Arg..." I turn, sweeping our surroundings with a glance. Where is the rotten devil? I can't see him. His scent fades and then comes again. Gods, I hate vampires.

"I'm afraid he's right, darling." The voice is smooth as velvet, drifting in the night. Still no sign of him. "I've kept my eye on you for a very long time..."

A snarl. "Do you have any idea of how enticing your blood is? The scent is driving me mad!"

I shoot up one eyebrow and tilt my head. *Yeah... I can relate.*

Every certainty flees from the woman as her face pales with sheer black fright. Shuddering hazel eyes fix on mine for reassurance.

I step closer to her, carefully, and raise an appeasing hand while my gaze drifts to the trees. "Where the hell are you?" I mutter.

"Nobody's gonna snatch you away from me!" he spits.

The woman screams. The sound jolts my heart into a wild gallop. I look back and see the blood demon standing behind her, gripping her in his claws, lethal fangs flashing in the twilight, ready to stab his victim's neck.

Time slows down. Shifting will do nothing to stop him. I'll have to take other measures. I really shouldn't... Fuck. In a flash, my hand swings up at my eye level. I feel the surge of energy rushing through my limbs, unstoppable as it streams through my arms and beams off my palm. Spectral blue light gathers in my hand. I launch the magic sphere at the demon, spearing across the dark, until it strikes the vampire's head. The creature instantly drops to the ground, unconscious.

At least she didn't see it. The woman crashes to her knees, shaking as the purest dread consumes her. Dammit. None of this should have happened.

I release a quick breath and walk to the creature. Towering over the vampire, I tip my head. My bear demands blood and vengeance. Slowly, I crouch before him.

"Wait…" Her soft voice cracks the stillness.

The woman's gentle hand lands on my shoulder. At her touch, a bolt of lightning shoots through my limbs, shaking me so hard that I jerk back. Her widened eyes and quivering hands tell me she felt it too.

"What are you gonna do?" she asks.

"Kill him," I say dryly, still stunned by the blow.

Panic flits across her countenance. "What? Wait… Is there no other way?" she says, wringing her wrist with her hand. "Can't we just… let him go?"

My expression slips into a frown. Is she being serious? But then a voice speaks in my mind. *She's human. She knows nothing about a vampire's obsessive nature.* I stare at her with cool eyes, subdued by the power she unknowingly holds over me. I shake my head. The air burns as it rushes through my nose and into my lungs. "He will never stop," I say between quick breaths. "Not until he kills you."

"Oh God," she says under her breath, worry creasing her brow. She's losing it. Her cheeks burn red scarlet, and her eyes fill with tears. "Oh my God… I can't…"

"Look away," I tell her in a dispassionate tone.

Her glistening eyes search mine for reassurance. I give her that with a swift nod.

She steps back and shuts her eyes. "Oh God…" she says with a strained voice, fingers diving through her golden locks of hair.

"Don't open your eyes," I say under my breath. The bones crack when I crush the vampire's neck. My claws break beneath my fingernails. One quick sweep severs the demon's head. The claws gradually retract, and my hand becomes human again.

Now to get rid of the body. I don't want her to see this mess.

I hold my hands open, palms facing head and corpse. "*Evanescet*," I say under my breath, exhausted. Within seconds, the remains burst into myriad glowing embers that soon fade into the darkness, taking away any traces of blood and gore. I rarely resort to this type of incantation. But for her, I would do anything.

Finally, I look at her. She stands in front of me, shuddering while she hugs her arms, eyes closed as she bites her lower lip. I am on my knees, watching her in absolute awe. She doesn't even begin to suspect that I am at her mercy.

4

LUCIANA

*C*old embraces me inside out. I can't stop trembling. My heart is about to explode. Did I really just see Trent grow fangs? God, he tried to bite me. He tried to *kill* me! Dear God, and this man—he leapt out of the woods and saved my life. And when he touched me, he all but zapped me with an electric burst of energy. I think he tased Trent. Maybe that's what set off some static between us?

This can't be real, but it is. I saw these things with my own eyes. And Trent... Oh God! I bury my face in my hands.

"You can open your eyes now," the stranger says. His voice is low and gentle, as if he fears I might break. Who am I kidding? I'm a mess. My mind is spinning like crazy.

I'm afraid to open my eyes, but I swallow hard and do as he says. The first thing I see is him standing in front of me. My head swings up to meet his dark brown eyes, enhanced by the shadow of his short boxed beard. The guy is tall and burly, a little over six feet. His chestnut hair is long, tied back into a low bun.

My gaze travels lower, to the damp white shirt sticking to his firm chest and chiseled abs. I flush and look down fast.

Stop staring at him, Luciana! What's the matter with you? You almost died a minute ago, and this man saved you. And he killed Trent, who was a vampire! My breaths become short and rapid. Warm tears blur my vision, frantic, as I look behind the man. Where's Trent's body? Where is...?

The stranger holds me by the shoulders. My arms tingle at his touch. I can't control it. "Look at me," he says, and I jump at the sound of his voice. "Don't look for him. Look at me."

I do as he says, fear and confusion knotting inside me.

"You're overwhelmed right now," he continues in a low, soothing voice. "You shouldn't have seen any of this. But you did. And I'm sorry. And it's over now." He stops to catch his quickened breath.

I take a hand to my lips. "Trent, he was…" I shudder. "He was… Where is he?" I'm afraid he might jump out of the trees again and get me this time.

"Gone," he says, boring his serene eyes into my own. "There's no coming back from where he is. You are safe." He does not falter as he says these things.

I want to believe him, but I sweep the grounds with a glance, anyway. There's not a trace of Trent. It's as if he'd vanished altogether. But then, he was a vampire. Maybe that's what happens when you kill a vampire? Oh God! I can't believe this is happening!

"Let me take you home," he says, leaning down until our stares level.

My brow creases with bemusement. A storm of emotions breaks inside me. "But he was…" I find myself speaking in the lowest of voices. I still feel like Trent might come back and kill me. "He was taking me home." My lips quiver. I'm on the brink of tearing up. "And I don't… I don't even know you!"

"I will *never* hurt you." He speaks with stern determination, so fiercely, it echoes as a solemn vow.

"No," I breathe, stepping back. "I can't… I'll be okay on my own…" If I've learned anything in the past few minutes is to be wary of the people who surround me.

As I walk to the gates, the man stands still in the middle of the road. His eyes follow me until I reach the sidewalk. I grab my phone out of my purse and speed-dial Marco. He doesn't pick up, probably mad at me still.

My heart is racing, but I push my steps into a trot. I need to get home. I need to take a shower. And then, find a therapist.

5

GAVRIIL

I let her go. Against every fiber in my being, screaming I should grab her and make her mine, I let her leave. *She's human.* I scream at myself. *She's a woman. Not a witch or a shifter.* I should not feel such a powerful pull towards her. I'm a warlock and a bear shifter. Humans have no part in my world. Dallying with one is not only forbidden, but it goes against everything I stand for. And besides, the last time I belonged to someone, she died, and it almost got me killed. So no. No more dating for me... I can't stop thinking about her, though.

I am the fucking King of the Ursa Clan, for crying out loud. I should be able to master my emotions.

I should have enchanted her, made her forget about this incident. But I did not. And I fear I skipped this vital step because removing the vampire's recollection would have erased all memory of me as well. And I *do not* want her to forget about me. I want to stay engraved in her memory, even if that means being tied to hatred. Even if she resents me for annihilating her vampire date.

"Argh…" I growl. One deep breath and I start to walk to the park's gates. I need to get away from her scent. I gave her enough of a head start. It shouldn't be a problem. I'll hit the gym and take a cold shower. Dammit, I feel bitter. So much for my first day in Rome… Perhaps I should not have meddled. But the truth is I do not regret it.

The woman's face is stuck in my mind and I cannot stop picturing it as I make my way back home. After a twenty-minute walk, I make it out of Via Pomarancio and turn right into Via Monte Parioli, when the unexpected happens.

I see her. *Her.* She's walking on the opposite sidewalk. My heart jolts into a quickened beat. Is she following me? "Oh gods…" I mumble, rolling my eyes back. Just when I thought I'd never see her again.

The woman senses my piercing stare. Her eyes fly

open when she notices me. I expect her to be startled and ashamed, caught in her spying game. But she's not. Why else would she be around here? She's following me. I guess I really made that great of an impression…

She glowers at me. "Stop following me," she says.

I halt, astounded. "What?" I frown.

She stops too. "Stop. Following. Me." Her voice is hoarse with frustration.

I stiffen, as though she's struck me. "I am absolutely NOT following you." The words sail through clenched teeth. "*You're* following *me!*"

The corner of her lips twist in utter exasperation. She folds her arms over her chest. And now we're screaming at each other across the street.

"*Silenzio!*" Someone silences us from a window above.

I swing my head forward, away from her, and keep moving on the sidewalk. The woman's scent is completely overwhelming; but somehow, my anger subdues my impulse to cross the street and shut her mouth with a passionate kiss.

Stop thinking about her. But how can I? She's across the street, moving in the same direction as I am! Why is she doing this? Is she torturing me on purpose? Where is Sasha? I need him to come to my rescue.

The front lawn's cypress trees rise a few feet ahead. The minute I reach the gates, I press the intercom. I do not want to linger here longer than necessary. I'm suffering enough as it is, having her so near. The butler buzzes me in as soon as he sees me through the camera. I push the gate open, but I can't stop myself, and I look across the street one more time before I step inside.

The woman is standing at the same street level as me, house keys in hand, and that fearsome bag strapped on her shoulder. She glares at me, biting the inside of her cheek. "You have got to be kidding me," she says in a low voice, inescapable to my sharp senses.

"What now?" I snap, arms wide, palms facing skyward. Ever since I met her, she's been impossibly rude. Not to mention, she hasn't even thanked me for saving her life. "Does my home offend you?"

She exhales sharply and shakes her head a little. The woman then turns around, facing the gates that stood behind her. Her delicate hand enters a code into the buzzer. The gates open.

"Son of a...." The words drift into silence. "You

live there." I gasp in undiluted disbelief. My expression remains as flat as my tone.

Her hazel eyes fix on mine. She's no longer glowering, so there's that. She simply nods.

Fuck. This is a nightmare. My gaze shoots skyward, sweeping the five-floored building that rises behind her. I wonder which one is her apartment... *No. Stop. Don't think about that. You've got to stop thinking about this woman, no matter how alluring her scent is!*

That's it. I'm moving out of here.

"Stay safe," I tell her as offhandedly as I can, immediately regretting every single word. What's the matter with me? *Stay safe?* I could have done so much better than that.

"Gavriil," a voice calls from the intercom's speaker. "Are you coming in?" It's Sasha. He speaks in Russian.

The woman hesitates while pushing the gates further.

"In a minute," I tell him in English. One last look at this gorgeous woman. "Good night, I guess." I shrug my shoulders.

When I face my gates once more, my expression slips into a painful frown. I wince. Ugh. I want to bang my head against the iron bars, but I figure I've frightened this woman enough for a single evening.

And then, the unforeseen happens. "Good night," she says. Her voice is soft and warm. Not at all angry. "Neighbor," she adds.

My heart stops. I subtly turn her way and stare at her with uncertainty. *Leave now, Gavriil. Walk away before you say more stupid nonsense.*

I give her a quick nod and cross the gates fast.

Luciana
Marino

6

GAVRIIL

I lie on the bed, not even under the sheets, because I know covering myself would be completely useless. One look at the bedside table and I read the time. 3 AM. I haven't been able to sleep, and I won't be able to sleep. Not when I know she's but a few feet away from my reach. Why could she not live on the other side of the Tiber, or better yet, in another city? Florence would be nice. Anywhere, really. Now I'm just rambling...

"Gavriil."

The mellow voice comes from the doorway. I turn and find Sasha, tall and strong, leaning against the door jamb. He's giving me *that look*. I hate when he gives me that knowing look.

"What is it?" I mumble, avoiding his stare.

Out of the corner of my eye, I see Sasha slip his hands into his pants pockets. "Gavriil, I like to believe that other than your Enforcer and personal guard, I'm a good friend of yours."

"Of course we're friends," I mumble, grabbing my cellphone as a distraction. I'm scrolling through my emails, not really caring enough to even read the words. "I thought that would be clear by now, especially after what happened."

"Yeah… We should talk about that," he adds in a whisper.

I drop the phone beside me and throw a full glare at my Enforcer. "What is there to talk about, Sasha?" The bear in me bristles. I rise from the bed and move to the window. "Dating Bella was a mistake. I should have known better… I risked my crown for her and all for what? In the end, she betrayed me with Grisha." A pause. "I'll never forgive myself for being so foolish… Not a day passes that I do not regret meeting her. Is that what you want to hear me say?"

I catch his reflection in the pane of glass. Sasha shakes his head. "It's been two years," he says, subdued. "You must stop…"

"Sasha, she's dead!" I growl, digging my nails into the windowsill. "Grisha killed her. And the fucking beast vanished." My chest heaves as undiluted fury rushes in my blood.

"We *will* find him, brother." For all the calmness in his tone, Sasha remains cautious, standing on the room's threshold. "I'm glad you're finally talking about it." He sighs. "Coming here was the best choice, after all."

Something catches my eye outside. My gaze narrows. "I'm not so sure about that…" I say, pulling the curtain aside. A man on a motorcycle pulls into the building's driveway. He climbs off the vehicle and approaches the gates.

Two more men strolling on the sidewalk turn into the street and join the first. I don't like this at all.

I crack the window open, hoping I might hear them, but they're absolutely silent. However…

"It's been almost a decade since you took some time off, Gavriil," my Enforcer says, stepping inside. Even then, I do not move. "This is exactly what you need."

"Sasha," I mumble, eyes locked on the fiends standing on the sidewalk.

"Yeah?" He stops beside me.

"There are three vampires outside," I say, slightly stepping back.

A low growl rumbles in Sasha's throat. "Pesky

blood demons," he mutters. "They're everywhere nowadays. How did they even find us?" He inches closer and looks through the window.

"I don't think they're after us," I tell him.

Sasha furrows his brow. "Wait," he says. "How do you know they're vampires? I see only three men gathered on the sidewalk."

I sneer. "Can't you smell the stench of blood sticking to their fangs?" I breathe in a menacing whisper. "Anyway, I know exactly why they're here..." Another step away from the window.

"Why?" he asks, facing me with distinct concern. Now he tilts his head. "What did you do, Gavriil?"

"I'll explain later." I slip on my shoes with haste and dash to the door. "Help me take care of them. She's in danger."

"She?" My Enforcer winces. "I understand absolutely nothing..." He dives his fingers through his blonde mane of hair. "But I don't have much of a choice now, do I?"

I look back. "You don't."

WRATH STREAMS THROUGH MY VEINS LIKE brushfire as I cross the street. "What business do you have here?" I demand the minute I reach the blood fiends. My hands are free, ready to strike if it comes to it. Sasha stands beside me.

The blood demons start and look back. The preternatural gleam in their cunning eyes gives away their nature in an instant. "Human…" the leader mutters in the lowest voice. The sound drifts unhindered to my heightened hearing.

"Go away now," he says in Italian. "You don't want to be here." The creature's pupils widen as they fix on me. But a vampire's persuasion does not work on warlocks.

"I don't think you understand…" Sasha says, moving closer. In a flash, he stands behind the blood drinker, a powerful arm wrapped around its throat, a hand seizing the creature's jaw. He twists hard and fast, breaking the vampire's neck. One more jerk, and the head comes off.

The third vampire shrieks in undiluted horror and disappears into thin air. Sasha drops the head on the pavement and grabs the vampire leader before he gets a chance to flee. "The King asked you a straightforward question," Sasha speaks into the demon's ear. "He deserves a straightforward answer."

I step closer, skipping the pool of blood that stains the sidewalk.

"The... K-king?" The blood drinker writhes under my Enforcer's fearsome hold.

I stop inches away from the demon. "So much for a vampire's loyalty..." I sneer. "You're all alone now. Tell me why you're here, and I will let you go." My voice comes low and cold.

The creature hisses like a wild animal. He tries to become free from Sasha's grip. In vain, for my Enforcer's strength is no match for his. "I'll tell you nothing!" He grins, flashing his sharp fangs at me.

Sasha locks an arm around the creature's neck. I hope he doesn't kill him yet, but if he does, I won't hold it against him. The world would be a better place if rid of vampires.

"It's Your Majesty," Sasha hisses in the monster's ear.

I lean down a little, leveling my stare with the vampire. Magic stirs in my core. It flows through my limbs. I feel its warmth prickling my skin, filling me in powerful, unrelenting waves. My eyes burn with blue spectral flames each time this happens.

My fangs slowly drop. I flash them at the blood demon with half a smile. "You're not the only one with fangs around here..." I all but hiss.

"Who are you?" The blood drinker's eyes shudder as sheer black fright washes over him.

"My name is Gavriil Alexeev," I whisper, inching closer.

"The Ursa King!" he stammers, visibly shaking now. I do not pretend to deny the unfortunate fame that precedes my name.

"Tell me why you're here," I remind him.

"You're a bear shifter. You should know the answer!" the vampire all but spits. The creature's pale expression slips into a grimace of contempt. "Did you do it? Did you kill Trent?"

I tilt my head and stare at him, bemused. Trent. It rings a bell. "I did," I tell him with the same dispassionate tone.

Behind the vampire, Sasha's eyes fly open. He watches me in undiluted shock.

"So, you found him..." I continue.

"Oh, yes. We saw what you did to him!" The demon groans as Sasha's grip tightens. My Enforcer's ice-blue eyes lock on mine for approval. I raise a hand, ordering him to wait.

An eerie cackle sails through the creature's crooked lips.

"What's so funny?" Sasha growls, forcing his arm harder against the vampire's neck.

"You don't even know..." Another wicked laugh. "Trent was sired by Andrea Barone," the vampire says, smirking proudly. "He will hunt you down until he's finished you both!"

I exhale roughly. My patience grows thin. "What do you want with the woman?" I roar. "She played no part in this."

The vampire scowls. "Don't you know?" he replies in reckless fury.

"Answer him!" Sasha presses, ready to snatch the vampire's head off.

A whimper escapes the creature's mouth. "The woman's blood is unique!" he says in a blurt. "*Sangue d'Oro.* No one dared come after her when Trent was around. But now that he's gone…"

I step back, taken by the blow of the monster's revelation. *Sangue d'Oro.* Gold Blood, ambrosia to any vampire. This is worse than I thought. I turn to my friend with intent. "Sasha…" I breathe. He understands. "Let him go."

The creature gasps for air as soon as Sasha relaxes his grip.

I draw closer to the fiend, ardent fury coursing through my limbs. "You will never touch her," I mutter. "None of you will."

Relief gives way to panicked bemusement on the monster's face.

"Start. Running," I growl through clenched teeth.

My fierce gaze cuts to my Enforcer's. Sasha nods.

The second the vampire flees, dashing through the night like the vilest shadow, Sasha darts after him. As my Enforcer sprints towards the end of the street, he gradually shifts into his bear form. Claws break beneath his fingernails, pristine white hair covers his arms... The blood drinker won't make it far before Sasha destroys him.

I turn to the apartment building. Tracking the woman won't be a problem. Her sweet scent lures me like a bee to a honeycomb. This isn't the last of the vampires we'll see. More will follow.

I must warn her.

7

LUCIANA

’ve been staring at the ceiling for the past hour. I don't think I'll be able to sleep tonight—or ever again. Trent was a vampire. A vampire. He tried to kill me. If vampires are real, then what else is out there? And then there's my *hot neighbor*. The guy is drilled into my brain. How did he know Trent wasn't human?

I will never harm you, he said. Shivers spread through my limbs as I remember the intensity of his stare, his sheer conviction as he spoke the words.

"Gah!" I push the covers away. I'm not falling asleep anytime soon. I gather my hair into a quick high bun and drag my bare feet out of bed and into the kitchen.

"Tea," I mumble, opening the cabinet. Save for the can of tea and some sugar packets, the cupboard is practically empty. I should do some grocery shopping. People need food to survive, don't they? Ugh. I open the can and grab a spoon and a cup.

Someone knocks at the door.

Huh? I look at the clock. 3:45 AM. Who would come knocking at this hour? Oh, I know. It's that pesky woman from the apartment downstairs. The last time she had a grievance, she pulled the same thing on me. I clench my jaw. Who does she think she is? Does she think I'm a 24-hour customer service and she can come whenever something ticks her off? I march out of the kitchen and into the hallway. Last time, I was nice. But not tonight.

"You're gonna get an earful, Glenda..." I mutter, closing my hand on the doorknob. I jerk the door open and am faced with long chestnut hair, dark brown eyes rimmed with thick black eyelashes, a sculpted nose and lips.

My stomach drops.

It's him. Hot Neighbor.

On an impulse, I shut the door. My heart is pounding hard against my chest. I cover my mouth with my hand and press my back against the wall, knees trembling, hands clammy as hell. Was it really him? How?

"Please open this door," Hot Neighbor says in a dispassionate tone.

A thrill spreads through my limbs. A dozen questions race through my mind, but I choose one fast. "What do you want?" I tell him, struggling to master the restlessness crashing inside me.

"We need to talk," he says. "It's important." Now his voice is strained with worry.

He sounds serious. I do as he says. He stares at me with impassible eyes. His gaze drops from my face to my legs. Only then, I realize I'm wearing nothing but a t-shirt. *Crap.*

Hot Neighbor's stare lands in my eyes again. "You'll have to change," he says in the same sober voice. "It's cold outside."

The last remark hits me. "What?" I flinch.

"You're coming with me," he says, as if it were obvious. Well, it's not.

Now I glare at him. "I am not—!"

"You can't stay here." He halts, looking away for a second. "Gods, I don't even know your name…" he muses, creasing his brow into a deep frown.

"It's Luciana…" I tell him in a gentler disposition.

"Good," he says with quiet assurance. His stare burns through me. "Luciana, your recently deceased vampire boyfriend had many friends. *Powerful* friends."

A soft gasp escapes my lips. "He wasn't my—"

"They came to kill you," he cuts me off. "My friend Sasha is dealing with them now."

Crushed ice fleets down my nape. "What?" I manage as the air in my throat freezes.

"Please go change, and pack your essentials," he insists. His gaze shoots skyward, and he glides his fingers through his long mane of hair. He releases a long breath when he looks at me again. Wow. It looks like he's really struggling over there. No idea why. "You're staying with me for a while."

What in the...? My lips part, ready to speak the words, but no sound comes through.

He straightens. "You'll have to stay with me. Otherwise, I won't be able to protect you," he adds with a curt demeanor.

I scowl. "I can take care of myself..."

His hand points down the hallway. "There's an entire vampire coven after our heads, woman." A twinge of frustration laces his voice. "So whatever beef you've got with me, I suggest we solve it quickly."

His readiness spikes my anxiety. "None of this would have happened had you not jumped at us in the park!" I say in a blurt. I breathe in short, shallow breaths, unable to control the spasmodic trembling inside me.

"You would be dead right now if I hadn't," he says, holding back his temper. No arrogance seeps through his tone. He's simply stating a fact. And that shuts me up. For a while, at least.

His eyes bore into mine. "Luciana..." The way he says my name makes everything inside me stop. Every thought freezes, my breathing halts, my pulse chokes for a precious instant. My body goes taut.

Last time he warned me and I didn't listen, it almost got me killed. I bite my lower lip. I'm not taking any chances now. "Uh… okay," I manage, opening the door wider. "It'll just be a moment. Come in."

He's almost as tall as the doorframe. Handsome in dark denim, a black t-shirt, and a black leather jacket. "We should hurry," he says, lingering at the entrance. "Go on."

Wordless, I nod. My pulse is racing. I barely catch my breath by the minute I make it to the bedroom. With quivering hands, I grab a gym bag and stuff it with a few changes of clothes, shoes. Then I dash to the bathroom and grab everything I'd take with me on a weekend break… although this sounds like anything but that.

8

GAVRIIL

uck. How will I be able to resist her? It's taken all of my self-control not to jump on her and devour her with sultry kisses. My inner bear does not listen to sense or reason. It wants what it wants. I don't think it's ever yelled at me with such harsh determination. I don't think I've ever felt like this before. Not even with Bella… This is going to be hard as hell. But there's no other way I can protect her.

"You haven't told me your name…" Luciana says. Her tone is sweet. *Luciana*. Even her name is lovely.

Double fuck.

"It's Gavriil," I say with reluctance.

"Oh…" I see her stop in the middle of the bedroom. Luciana slips on a pair of jeans. She's tugging on the trim of her oversized t-shirt. She's going to take it off.

For the love of Chernobog. Against my bear's claims, I look away. She has absolutely no idea of the torment I'm going through right now. I shut my eyes and pray to all the gods that the woman dresses quickly.

"Are you…?" she asks.

"Are you ready?" I interrupt. Everything in this room is redolent of her enticing fragrance. Foolishly, I try to convince myself it'll get easier once we're in my home, which is a large estate. But still. I know it won't make a difference.

"*Che cavolo…*" Luciana mutters in the lowest of voices, but my hearing picks it up. She's crossed at me for my brashness, but her voice is so tender I can't stop myself from smiling and shaking my head. *I'm so screwed.*

Finally, she zips up her bag. "Ready as I can be," she says, standing at the bedroom's doorway.

I straighten. "Great. Let's go."

WE HURRY OUT OF THE ELEVATOR. WORD OF mouth spreads rapidly between immortals. I'm sure we'll hear from them soon enough.

"Come on," I urge her as we cross the building's gates. I move forward, but Luciana lags behind.

"Is that…?" she mumbles.

When I look back, her widened eyes stare at the pool of blood on the pavement. *Dammit, I forgot about that.* At least the vampire's remains are gone.

She turns to me, pale and sickly. I catch her in my arms fast, seconds before she hits the ground. "Luciana…" Slowly, her starry eyes fix on mine. I promised myself I wouldn't do this, but… I press two fingers on her forehead. "*Obliviscor,*" I whisper, erasing that bit of memory.

Instantly, she faints.

With no time to lose, I flash my palm at the sidewalk, summoning my ancestral magic. Spectral blue light shoots off my hand and covers the demon's blood, evaporating it within seconds. Gods, how could I forget to clean up? That was sloppy of me. But then, everything in me has felt messed up ever since I met this woman.

I lift her, weightless, in my arms, and carry her home.

9

LUCIANA

Twilight spreads in the room when I open my eyes. I see white stuccoed ceilings detailed with baroque paintings of the horned god, Bacchus, and Ariadne. The story comes to me, how Bacchus fell in love with Ariadne and made her his wife… Instant love. Am I delirious?

Wait a minute. Where am I?

"You're awake," a soft voice says. It's gentle as a low croon, a purr that makes my skin prickle with waves of pleasure. My eyes begin to close again.

"Luciana," he says, bringing me back.

I remember him suddenly. A soft gasp leaves my mouth. "Gavriil…" My head swings to the side lazily, and I meet the man's dark, brooding eyes. He stares at me, uncertain. He's sitting on a chair next to the bed. This must be his home.

"God," I mumble, furrowing my brow. "I don't know what happened to me." I force myself to remember, but it only gives me a headache. "We were leaving my apartment and I just…" I take a hand to my forehead.

"You fainted," he says. "I shouldn't have rushed you."

That sounds about right. I try to sit up on the bed. My limbs feel soft and shaky. Gavriil approaches a hand towards me with caution, as though he fears I might bite it off. I would have, before. But not now.

He carefully holds my arm. A shiver ripples through me at his touch. Finally, I manage to sit.

"My friend Sasha brought you some tea and biscuits," Gavriil says, still leery. Is he afraid of me? Why would he be? Out of the two of us, he's the one who's tall and muscular, and so handsome… *Snap out of it, Luciana.* I shake my head, trying to shed those thoughts for now.

"You said there were more?" I stammer, fear clenching my throat. I don't want to speak of this, but I have to know. "That they came to kill me, but your friend Sasha took care of them?" Slowly, my mind rebuilds those memories.

Gavriil nods. He's not much of a talker, is he? My brow tangles with worry. "You stopped Trent when he tried to kill me," I begin. "Are you like, a vampire hunter? Like, uh… Buffy?" I immediately regret saying that. *All* of that. Inside, I'm screaming at myself and wincing.

He leans closer, intrigued. "Who's Buffy?" he asks.

"You don't know?" I blurt. How can he not know? Does he live under a rock when he's not in Rome?

"Gavriil…" a man says. He stands at the bedroom's doorway. He's tall and of a muscular build, with a medium-length blonde mane of hair and striking ice-blue eyes.

Gavriil rises. "Sasha," he says, and meets him at the door.

They talk in the lowest of voices, but I can still listen to their conversation. They do not speak in English, however. At one point, Gavriil nods. He pats his friend's arm and then returns to the chair by my side while his friend leaves.

"I am not a vampire hunter," he continues, easing my restlessness. "I'm a…" he hesitates. Why does he falter? "I'm the head of my family. There's a lot worse than vampires where I come from."

"And where is that?" I ask with no restraint.

"Saint Petersburg." He replies quickly, eagerly.

"Oh, that's right. Your name.... I wasn't sure that's what it was," I say. "And just now, you were speaking Russian then." I grab the cup from the nightstand and take a swig of tea. Apple cinnamon. My favorite.

"Yeah, sorry about that." Gavriil shrugs. "I've ordered Sasha to stick with English for as long as you're here, but…"

"*Ordered* him?" I raise my brow. "So, he's your—"

Gavriil shifts in his seat. "He's my…" He clears his throat.

"Personal assistant," I add knowingly. The house is pretty luxurious. It makes sense he'd have one.

"Yeah." Another fast response. Gavriil smooths his long hands over his knees and lets out a brief exhalation.

"You might not be a vampire hunter, but I bet you kill your fair share of vampires back in Saint Petersburg…" I mumble.

Gavriil slightly creases his brow. "We don't have any."

"Huh?"

"Listen… you might want to let your family know that you'll take a few days off."

"I don't have one," I tell him in all honesty. "All I had left was my grandfather, and he died a little over a year ago."

"Oh… Maybe work then." Again, he moves in the seat. He's a rather large hunk for such a delicate chair. But I don't think that's what makes him uncomfortable. I think it's me. But why? Well, I did hit him hard with my bag.

"You should let your boss know that… uh…"

"I'm the boss." My lips stretch into an easy smile. "I'll text my friend Marco and have him take over the shop for a few days." Suddenly, staying with Gavriil doesn't seem as daunting as it did when he came knocking. He's shown me nothing but kindness ever since we met. And he's a vampire killer. The closer I have him, the better.

It then dawns on me. He risked his own life to save mine. Gavriil didn't even know me. I almost died back there. He's about to stand when my hand seizes his. "I'm sorry," I tell him wholeheartedly.

His hand stiffens beneath mine. Gavriil's dark brown eyes slightly widen. His breathing halts.

"I should have thanked you," I confess, stricken with worry. My gaze captures his. "I'm apologizing now for behaving like such a bitch back then." I stare at our hands. Why am I holding him? "God… I even hit you."

"No apologies needed," he says, taking my hand

to my lap. He does it with such delicacy it makes my wrist tingle all the way up to my arm.

"You should rest." Breathless, Gavriil rises from the chair. He reaches the entrance in three long strides. "Let me or Sasha know if you need anything." He stops at the doorway to look back. "I'll see you at dinner."

Dinner? Was I out of it that long? I look at the windows. They're covered with blackout curtains. "Sure," I tell him.

He nods and walks out of the room.

I take one long sip of tea. Its warmth fills me in an instant. Like a hug that sweeps away my fears and wraps me with cozy, loving feelings. It's almost like… magic.

My heart is about to explode as I march downstairs. I don't know how I'm going to be able to survive this, having Luciana so close. I seek refuge in my library. Books are the mind's haven. Anyone who thinks differently makes me suspicious.

When I open the door, I see Sasha. He lounges on the couch by the hearth, staring at his cellphone with an inscrutable expression.

"What do we know so far?" I ask him while I move across the room.

Sasha straightens in the seat. His fierce blue eyes follow me until I sit behind the desk. "I made a bit of research about what that blood demon said."

"*Sangue d'Oro?*" I raise my brow. "What did you learn?"

"Apparently, Gold Blood is an extremely rare blood type. Usually, it's found within old families..." Sasha puts the phone away, focusing his attention on me. "Vampires crave it. It's a most coveted experience, and you know how bored vampires can get."

"Filthy demons..." I mutter, looking away.

"Anyway," my Enforcer continues, "the woman has it, and—"

"Luciana," I interrupt him.

He frowns. "Huh?"

"Her name is Luciana," I add. My mind whirls, stuck in the moment when she grabbed my hand. *Release me,* I wanted to growl back then. *We're close enough as it is!* She does not realize that her sole touch unleashes a storm of emotions inside me. As if being a warlock and a shifter weren't enough, I am an Empath. It's not something I can turn on and off at sheer will.

For an ordinary human, Luciana bears loads of energy. Her radiance is simply sublime.

Do not fall for her, I remind myself. When I first caught her scent, I thought it wouldn't be more than a onetime fling. But she's proven me wrong time and time again ever since. And the more we talk, the more

I realize I am in danger of falling in love with her... I can't. I suffered enough the last time that happened. My heart cannot bear another wound. But what if I opened my heart one last time?

"No!" I growl, swinging my head to the side.

"Gavriil?" Sasha says in a low voice. He leans forward, his face twisted into a grimace of worry. "Are you all right?"

"I'm fine," I say under my breath, pulling the drawer open. There's a bottle of whiskey and a glass. I pour myself a drink.

"Are you sure, brother?" He rises from the seat.

"I'm fine, Sasha," I mutter, pushing away the glass. "Everything's fine!"

I can read the startled confusion in my friend's expression. But I do not care to elaborate, and he knows better than to insist.

Sasha moves to the desk and stops there, silent for a couple of minutes. He sucks in one deep breath and releases it slowly. "I think we should call in our brothers," he finally says.

My gaze glides to his. "No..." This time, I all but plead.

"If you want Luciana to be safe, we'll have to stand up to these vampires at some point," he continues, speaking to me in a paused soothing tone. "We'll need more men."

I hate that he's right. If it were up to me, I'd keep things simple. But Luciana's life is at stake. My desires matter little. A sigh sails through my lips. "Just the Elite," I breathe. "No more."

"The Elite team should be more than enough," my Enforcer says, pulling his phone out of his jacket's pocket. He moves to the terrace, ready to make the call.

I turn to my laptop's screen and look at the keyboard with an empty stare. Then, after a moment's thought, I sluggishly type in the letters *B-U-F-F-Y.*

"Gavriil?" a voice says.

My head swings up and meets her standing at the doorway. My pulse skyrockets in an instant. Gods, will I ever stop feeling like I'm walking on the edge of a cliff every time I see her?

I spring off the seat. "Hey," is all that comes out of my mouth. *I'm such an idiot.* "How are you doing?" *That's better.* I close the laptop.

"Good," she says, still lingering by the threshold. *Please, stay there.*

She gathers her hands, hesitant to speak while she picks at her nails. "Have any of them come back?"

Should I tell her I set up security cameras shooting at her apartment and the building's entrance? No. That would make me come off as a tad overprotective of the people I care about—which I am, for the most part. But she doesn't have to know that. Not yet, anyway.

"They haven't," is all I say. "I don't think they'll come back until they've come up with a plan."

She has not moved an inch. Neither have I. The air thickens, saturated with our energies. Tension and lust on my part, anxiety on hers. I can all but touch her feelings.

I do not wish to frighten her, so I spare her the details of a vampire's schemes. Blood drinkers are vicious creatures. They will always strive to get what they want, especially when blood is concerned. They usually resort to damaging a victim's family or loved ones to get their way, which is why I took the precaution of asking if she had any living relatives. Fortunately, she does not.

Even when I've carefully omitted that piece of information, her face still pales in dismay. A wild impulse to hold her rises in me. I press my hands on the desk, anchoring myself to the slab of wood. It takes everything inside me not to leap over it and comfort her.

When her gaze drifts to the axes displayed on the

wall, I push myself to speak. "Do you like them?" I ask like a fool.

"They're beautiful," she says, hugging her arms. "Do you collect axes?"

"I throw them." *Idiot.* I want to hide under the desk and never come out. "For sport," I add. This is so awkward… "Sasha's a wonderful cook," I blurt. *Good gods, what is the matter with me?* "He'll be making dinner for us tonight." A pause to steady my quickened breaths. "I… uh… sent the staff away. I hope that makes you more comfortable." I swallow hard. My mouth is as dry as the Sahara Desert.

"Thank you," she says in a low, timid voice.

"Feel free to roam about the house," I add. "Overall, it's pretty boring, but…"

"It's a beautiful home," she says with earnest hazel eyes.

"Yeah." I nod, pleased. The corner of my lips slightly curls up.

"Everything's settled," Sasha says, reentering the room. He notices Luciana's presence, and halts. Instinctively, he bows his head to her, then says, "Good afternoon."

"*Ciao*," Luciana says, unsure of how to behave. "You're Sasha…"

"Yes," he says, straightening as a light smile thins

his lips. "Nice to see you again, miss." He lowers his head, then shoots a knowing look at me before he leaves the room.

"I won't get in your way," she says. A crisp smile follows. "I'll see you at dinner."

You'd never get in my way, I want to tell her. "Yeah," I say instead. My sanity hangs from her every word.

Luciana turns and walks out of the library. The door closes behind her.

My lungs release with a hastened breath, and I shut my eyes, knowing myself doomed. Doomed, and in love with a human.

Aleksandr
(Sasha)

11

LUCIANA

The house was impressive from the outside. Inside, it's even bigger. I've spent the entire afternoon meandering through the vast halls, discovering its many rooms as if I wandered inside a museum. Frescoes reminiscent of the Titian decorate the ceilings. Bacchus and Ariadne are the constant themes. There are other references to mythology, like Venus and Mars, but not once have I spotted a Christian subject. It seems odd to me, but then Gavriil has often expressed himself in pagan terms. *Gods,* he says. I love the way he says it.

They say one can learn a lot about a person judging by their homes. Even if this is his summer home, I bet I can pick up more about Gavriil. For the time being, I can see he prefers order and having clear spaces. Even his desk was clean when I walked in. And the library, no clutter in sight... Good thing he didn't get to see my room.

My cellphone buzzes in my jeans back pocket. There's a message on the screen.

Marco: Everything all right, cara?

"Oh, now you care, Marco?" I mutter. Where was he when I needed him? I'm so angry at him. I put the phone away, back into my pocket. My stomach growls. I hope it's time for dinner soon.

At the end of the hallway, I glimpse a flood of amber light. I walk there, wondering what's beyond.

Tall glass doors open to the manor's garden. As I cross the threshold, I find a terrace with marble flooring. To my left, I see a small dining table, set up with white linens, candlelight, and glistening silverware. At the end of the terrace, Gavriil stands by the balustrade, looking over the gardens. Handsome in a spotless dark suit, hair combed back, tied into a low coil. He hasn't noticed me.

I look down at my ripped jeans and casual pullover. "I didn't bring any formal clothes..." I mumble. This guy comes from another world. A world of butlers, and PAs, and suits for dinner. I should have considered that.

He turns, his shoulders perfectly squared and hands slipped into his pants pockets. Gleaming maroon eyes. Gavriil's stare lingers on my face for a minute, then land on my own. A soft smile tugs at his lips. "You don't need any," he says simply.

My cheeks burn. For a minute, I think he meant I didn't need any clothes.

He takes a hand to his neck and loosens the tie until he slips it off. His fingers move swiftly to unbutton his shirt's neck. And all the while, I'm standing here, gawking at him. I can't help it. He's gorgeous.

Finally, he removes his jacket and tosses it over his shoulder. "Come on," he says, leading me to the table.

He pulls a chair for me. I sit, stunned, as I take in the beauty that surrounds us. "Do you always have dinner like this?" I ask, dumbfounded.

Gavriil grabs his seat. He silently stares at me for a minute. "Not always," he says in a low voice. "I thought you might enjoy the fresh air."

I smile. Smile like a fool. One quick glance at the table and I notice a set for two, a tray of artichoke and goat cheese bruschetta, insalata caprese, and two dishes covered with plate clochettes.

"Where's Sasha?" I ask. "Will he not dine with us?" I hear myself *poshing* out. Good grief. Am I that desperate for him to like me? I can't help it. He's usually so troubled and distant with me.

I suppose I should be grateful to carry those worries in my head, instead of actually panicking because a horde of vampires is after me. Vampires. It sounds so unreal. And yet, I saw Trent's fangs up close the minute he lunged at me in the park.

"He's already dined," Gavriil dismisses. "He had to leave early to… um… see some friends."

How guarded he is. I'm sure he's carefully omitting something. I might have figured him out. He's probably trying to protect me. "You can tell me," I suddenly say, certain that there's more.

Gavriil sighs. His expression relaxes as if he's taken a load off his chest. "I've asked a few friends to come over and… lend me a hand, just in case."

"In case the vampires come here looking for me." I complete the sentence.

The muscles in his neck stiffen and his jaw clenches tight. "Yeah…" he says, pulling the napkin off the table. He unfolds it with a quick shake and lays it on his lap.

I do the same.

There's so much about him I want to know. I vow to myself to dig up to the last secret out of him. But for now, I suck in one deep breath. "Okay," I tell him, trying to settle my emotions. "Let's eat."

When I uncover my plate, I see a steaming fillet mignon with a side of baked potatoes and asparagus parmigiano. It smells so good. I can't stop myself, and a moan escapes my mouth. I'm starving.

Gavriil cracks a smile. "Do you like it?" he asks, a hand on his plate cover.

"I sure do," I say in Italian, knife in hand, ready to dig in. Forget the salad and everything else.

He seems pleased. Gavriil cuts into his steak. And then I see. His cut of meat is seared beautifully on the outside, but practically raw inside. "Oh, yours isn't fully cooked," I tell him before he takes a bite. "We can share mine."

He shakes his head, impassible dark brown eyes fixed on me, twinkling garnets in the candlelight. "It's all right," he says in the smoothest voice.

Is it though? I shrug my shoulders. Some people like their steaks rare, I guess. I stack my fork with a slice of meat and potatoes and taste those. "Wow," I say. "Sasha cooked all this?"

"He did," he says in a quiet demeanor as he cuts another slice of meat.

"I can see why you keep him around…" I tease. Instantly, I become aware that I enjoy seeing him break from his self-possessed demeanor.

Gavriil gives me the hint of a smile. "He's a man of many talents," he says. "That's true."

At last, he seems a bit more relaxed. This is my chance. "So, these friends of yours," I begin in a casual tone, "are they coming from Saint Petersburg?"

"Some of them," he replies, looking down at his dish. Again, he becomes reserved and poised. "The rest are stationed nearby."

I start. "Stationed?" My mind reels with confusion. "Are they like, a military group?" A soft gasp sails through my lips. "Gavriil… I'm not understanding how—"

"They're my closest friends," he adds, giving no room for me to counter. His stare meets mine, steady and unwavering as ever. "I promise you will be safe."

"Sure…" I raise one eyebrow, unconvinced. "But for how long? I mean, I can't stay with you forever."

Gavriil says nothing. He lowers his gaze and continues to eat his meal. Minutes pass, and just when I'm about to become perfectly frustrated, he speaks again. "Tomorrow I shall take you to see a dear friend of mine," he says in the same dispassionate tone.

"Oh?" That's intriguing.

"She owns a coffee shop near the Pantheon," he continues, quirking a smile. "I think you'll like her."

"*Bene.*" I nod in agreement.

Gavriil narrows his eyes, watching me with undiluted wonder. "You're not going to ask me why I'm taking you to see her?" He leans slightly forward.

I shrug my shoulders. I leave the fork and knife on the table, place my hands on the sides of my plate, and stare at him. "You saved my life, Gavriil. Not once, but twice," I tell him. "If you want me to see your friend, I'm sure you have good reason for it."

"She's a witch." He tosses the words at me, elbows pressed on the table, fingers interlaced. And he watches me, ready to measure my reaction.

"A *strega?*" I raise my eyebrows. "My *nonna* was a *strega,*" I add dismissively. "Is she going to cast an enchantment to protect me from the vampires?"

Gavriil looks so shocked. The heavy lashes that shadow his cheeks fly up. He waits a minute until he speaks again. "I do not know." He speaks in all honesty. "We shall see tomorrow."

His gaze strays from me and angles to the terrace's entrance. I look back and notice Sasha standing quietly by the doorframe. "Luciana, will you excuse me?" he says, gathering the napkin and setting it on the table. Genuine concern looms on his face.

"Of course," I assure him.

He rises from the chair immediately. "Please, enjoy the rest of your meal," Gavriil says, then walks away.

12

GAVRIIL

I cannot read my brother's mind, but I know I'd find nothing but trouble if I could. The sole look in Sasha's eyes is enough to chill the blood in my veins. Wild fury mirrors in his stare. Something is terribly wrong.

Side by side, we march down the hallway, heading to the library. I see his clenched fists, the stiffness of his shoulders. "Gavriil…" he begins.

"Not here, Sasha," I warn him. The last thing I want is for Luciana to hear anything he has to say.

As soon as we close the doors behind us, I speak. "What is it?"

"It's worse than we thought," Sasha says, catching his breath. His frantic stare sweeps the ceiling, then drifts and finds mine. "When I summoned the Elite, out of the twenty, only twelve answered the call." He pauses, and I do my best not to interrupt him, but I fail.

"Our brothers in Rome," I add. "They answered the call."

"No." Sasha shakes his head. "Our brothers in Saint Petersburg are traveling here as we speak," he manages to say. "Our men stationed in Rome never replied."

"Why is that?" I press. My brow creases with worry.

"I asked myself the same question." He dips his hands into his pants pockets.

"And?" I urge him.

"I went to the safe house, and..." Sasha swallows hard. The anger in his expression slowly fades and gives way to dread. He's afraid to tell me the truth. Why?

"Sasha," I speak, not as a friend, but as his king.

His eyes rim with tears. "It was a bloodbath, Gavriil." He steps back and drops on the couch. "They're all dead."

Rage burns through me like molten lava. "Those fucking vampires!" I growl. Wave after wave of unhindered anger washes over me. I can't breathe. I can't think. Only the raw desire to see the blood demons destroyed pulses inside me. I would like nothing more than to tear this room apart, but what good would that do? The noise would frighten Luciana, for sure.

"Who's behind this?" I manage in a calmer voice, though my jaw clenches tight.

"Andrea Barone," Sasha says. "The leader of the Roman vampire coven."

My palms sting from digging my fingernails into them. "When will our brothers arrive?" I ask in a calmer voice.

"At around midnight."

I nod. "We're going to make him pay, Sasha," I tell him with a vacant stare, yet the clearest conviction. "We're going to skip the middle vamps and strike Barone himself when he least expects it." A pause. "But first, I must take Luciana to Natalya."

My Enforcer startles. "Natalya?" He springs from the seat. I read fright in his blue eyes, more than I noticed just a few minutes ago. Then it hits me.

"Oh, that's right…" I heave a sigh. "Listen, you don't have to come if you don't want to…"

Sasha harrumphs. "No," he says, finding his nerve again. "It's perfectly fine. I haven't seen her in a while, that's all."

"You can wait in the car, if you prefer…"

"Of course not." He speaks with sternness,

squaring his shoulders. "I have no problem with it. We cared for each other once. But that was a long time ago." He nods swiftly, slipping back into the role of my Enforcer. "I'll set up the team as soon as our brothers get here."

I stare at him sidelong.

"Luciana won't even know they're there," he assures me, fully aware of my concerns. "We will be discrete."

"Good," I say.

In silence, Sasha bows his head. He turns to the doorway.

"Sasha…"

He halts. "Yes, Your Majesty?"

"Tonight's dinner was superb," I tell him with a sullen voice, trying to smooth the dreariest mood. "Luciana passes her compliments to you."

He gives me a dry smile. "Perhaps I should have stuck with culinary school."

I shake my head. "Your *other* set of skills serve a better purpose with me," I say, leaning against the desk. "And they are much appreciated."

The smile on my Enforcer's lips slightly broadens. And for a split second, he looks like the young man of twenty-three that he is.

Sasha pulls the door open and leaves.

13

LUCIANA

It's 3 pm when Gavriil's driver drops us off at the Pantheon. Sasha steps out of the vehicle first. He sweeps the crowd with a glance, then opens the passenger door. Gavriil descends from the car. He dips his hands into his black wool coat and mimics Sasha's gesture, studying the horde of tourists with an appraising stare. Only then, he opens the door wider and allows me to come out.

It's a sunny afternoon, but October winds chill the narrow street where the shadows of the low sun creep fast. I'm so glad I brought a jacket with me.

Sasha stops beside the driver's window. He leans down a bit and whispers something into the man's ear. The driver silently agrees to whatever he's been told, and the silver BMW drives away.

The Piazza della Rotonda is crowded as usual. I find myself scanning through the faces that surround me, the same as Sasha and Gavriil… It then occurs to me. "Hey," I tell Gavriil.

His expression is stern when he eyes me sidelong.

"The sun is still up," I say. "Vampires only come out at night, so we should be safe, right?" I crack half a smile.

Gavriil exhales a long breath. He looks at the people, discarding friends from foes with a merciless glare. It shoots a sliver of ice down my nape.

My brow slips into a frown. "Right?" I insist as we move down the Via de Pastini.

Undiluted fierceness glints in his dark brown eyes when he looks at me again. The man is absolutely feral, with a mane of chestnut hair swaying in the breeze as we move, and an inextricable expression. He halts and pulls a door open. Without saying a word, he signals me to go inside.

I do as he says.

In a second, I'm engulfed in a bustle of overlapping conversations and porcelain cups clinking as they land on their saucers. "It's a coffee shop," I blurt. People eat pastries and drink espressos.

Vintage black and white photographs decorate the walls. Italian films from the sixties. I recognize

Marcello Mastroianni and Anita Ekberg, Ursula Andress and Sophia Loren.

Gavriil's hand suddenly folds in mine. A thrill rushes through my limbs at his touch. Never mind that he's not answering my question. His grip obliterates everything. I let myself go and follow him across the small coffee shop, dodging chairs, tables, and people moving in the opposite direction.

We head to the back of the shop, to an area with a sign that explicitly says "Employees Only". Well, he doesn't care, and he opens that door. I look over my shoulder. Sasha is always two steps behind us.

We cross the threshold into another world, it seems. The lights are dim. The walls are all draped in burgundy. Satin curtains frame the entrance to a long and narrow corridor.

When the door closes behind us, Sasha does not join us. He stays behind, in the coffee shop.

I follow Gavriil's steps when he halts without warning. I almost crash into him. We're standing so close, I can listen to his quickened breaths. When he turns, he inches close to me fast. My heart jolts at his nearness. The heavenly scent of his cologne floods my lungs. It's intoxicating in the most pleasurable way.

The space is so limited that when I move, my back presses against the wall. He leans forward even more. "Some vampires, especially very old ones, are capable of resisting broad daylight…" he whispers. His voice is laced with velvet that binds me and lures me to him. "You will be safe as long as I'm with you. I promise."

I nod. The minute he steps back, I breathe again. My pulse throbs hard in my ears and throat. I wonder if he can hear it. I feel he can hear it. It's silly. And yet… I flush like a fool.

When he releases my hand, it hurts a little.

I follow him. At the end of the hallway, we come to a door. The minute he pushes it open, I catch the sound of rippling waters. Between him and the door, I glimpse a small courtyard with a central fountain. Rosebushes and trees, stone benches set around the *fontana*.

As Gavriil meanders in the courtyard, a woman appears. She's young, no more than twenty-three. Her hair is golden brown, her eyes a stormy shade. She wears a bright green brocade mini skirt embroidered in gold, a clean-cut white shirt with sleeves folded just below the elbows, and high-heels.

"My darling!" she says in flawless Italian, opening her arms to him.

I feel my brow furrowing deeper. Who is this woman?

Gavriil beams with joy, as I've not seen him before. He returns the gesture, holding the woman in his muscular arms. He's happy and all I can feel is my stomach clenching.

"This is how I hear you're in town?" she scolds him with fondness. "You should have called sooner."

"Natalya," he tells her, moving aside so she can see me. "This is Luciana."

She scrutinizes me from head to toe. Her hard expression slowly thaws until finally, she smiles. I can tell it's genuine because her eyes smile too. "Come here," she tells me, opening her arms.

Oh, my. The *strega* is going to hug me. The thought of meeting her caused me no trouble last night. But now…

"She's shy…" she tells him. Gavriil's eyes are luminous when he looks at me. It's like seeing him for the first time, as the man he truly is. Free from all concerns regarding vampires, he's just a guy on vacation in Rome. A very handsome one.

Natalya comes to me and holds me in her arms. Her embrace is warm and caring, and it feels like she's my dearest friend, or family even. I yield to her hold, and she hugs me even tighter. Tears rim my eyes. What is she doing to me? Is this part of her magic? I can hear myself sobbing against her shoulder.

"There it is," she whispers in my ear. "Shed from all this pain, *cara*..." Natalya parts from me a little. Her delicate finger picks up one of my tears. She then takes her hand to the fountain. "And you will leave it here, in this fountain... *bene*?" The tear drops into the water.

Natalya's misty eyes lock on mine as she cups the sides of my face. Her smile is contagious. I wipe my tears away with my hands and nod.

"We need to work on you, Luciana. I would see you shed nothing but tears of joy," she assures me.

I sniff and accompany her through the courtyard. "That sounds wonderful," I tell her. God, she's better than a therapist. Maybe she is one.

As we walk past Gavriil, I look down, avoiding his stare. I'm so embarrassed that he saw me break like this. I can't face him right now.

"Gavriil?" Natalya says while she opens another door. "Are you coming?"

I hear his placid steps clank against the cobblestones. His alluring fragrance soon catches up with us.

We enter a kitchen. I'm wondering if she'll offer us some of that sublime espresso from the coffee shop. She moves further into the room, but I linger by the door and suddenly feel Gavriil standing right behind me. His presence is powerful, imbued with a magnetic pull that I find hard to resist... Is he aware of how he makes me feel? I doubt it. And right now, I feel like a complete fool.

Natalya gathers some herbs—rosemary, sage—and mashes them into a spray bottle, which she then fills with water. She tosses a pinch of salt in the mix, then adds a few drops of lemon oil. She now goes through the cabinet and takes out a small chest. As she opens it, she reveals dozens of quartz crystals, single ended, with a silver mounting ready for a chain.

"I brought Sasha with me," Gavriil suddenly says. His voice sends a thrill through my limbs and between my legs... *Stop it, woman. Maybe these herbs will strike some sense into you!*

Natalya drops everything. "Oh?" she utters, trying to regain her poise. She picks up the bottle and gives it a shake. "And, where is he?"

"Waiting for us," Gavriil says in a detached tone. "In the shop."

I move to the side, enough to see him as he leans against the door's jamb.

Natalya clears her throat. "That's nice," she says, returning to her strange cocktail. When she's finished, she closes the spray bottle and walks towards me. "I'm happy you're still friends."

Gavriil's brow creases into a frown. "Why would we not remain friends?" he asks, folding his arms over his chest.

"Because," Natalya stands before me, pointing the spray bottle at me as though it were a gun, "when he and I parted ways," she sprays my arms, "it was not in the *best*..." she sprays my chest and back and my legs, "*terms*," she mutters, spraying my face.

I scowl.

"Oh, my dear!" she says, mortified. "I'm so sorry!" Natalya covers her mouth with a hand. With the other, she reaches for a kitchen cloth and offers it to me. "Dab gently, please."

"Maybe this is not the best time for us to discuss this," Gavriil says in a low, playful tone.

I glare at him, stabbing him with my eyes. "Maybe not," I tell him, drying my face.

Natalya dashes to the counter and takes a silver chain, then slips two stones into it. When she comes back, she fastens the chain around my neck. "Black tourmaline and rose quartz, my dearest..." she mumbles. "You need them both."

Half my face is still wet when I point my cloth at

Gavriil. "You know, Natalya, I think *he* could use some magic spraying too."

Natalya's face brightens, pleased. She turns to Gavriil, bottle in hand. Her lips part, ready to speak when he interrupts her with, "No, no…" A dismissive hand in the air. "Thanks. I'm good."

She narrows her stormy eyes. "You're too good of a warlock for my spells, is that it?" she scolds him, a hand cinched to her waist.

His face slackens.

I crack a smile. "Oh, so you're a warlock *and* a vampire hunter?" I say, easing his restlessness. Given what I've been through in the last few days, him being a warlock is hardly disturbing.

Natalya stares at me, pleased. "I like her," she says. Now she turns to him. "I really do."

There's a moment of silence between us. This is so uncomfortable. The only thing missing is the chirp of crickets.

Natalya moves to the counter once more. She pulls a drawer open and extracts a small crystal container. It reminds me of the flasks where my *nonna* kept her perfume. Natalya opens the flask and pours the spray's liquid inside. When she closes it, I see the small pump pending from the cap. It's exactly like one of *nonna's* perfume dispensers.

"Now, take this," she tells me, handing me the bottle. "What vampires crave about you is your scent. Your blood's scent, actually. It permeates everything about you. They won't be able to track you as long as you wear this. With your scent covered, the vampires' craving will diminish." Her gaze cuts to Gavriil's. "*Everyone's* cravings will be subdued."

My brow tangles. I have no idea what she's saying. All I know is that this perfume will keep the vampires' fangs away from my neck, so that works for me.

"Thank you, Natalya…" Gavriil says, stepping outside.

She holds my arm and leads me to the courtyard. "Thank you," I tell her.

"Now, Luciana…" She faces me in confidence. "Remember, this is only a layer of protection. These vampires already know who you are, and they can still track you. So please," she holds my arms, "be careful."

"I will," I say.

Her lips stretch into a caring smile. *"Bene, bene…"* she says, and wraps me in a warm embrace. This time, I return her hug with the same affection.

"I'll talk to you soon," Gavriil says, opening the courtyard's door.

"You better." Natalya stands in the middle of the garden. "I'm your best cousin and you know it."

Gavriil smirks, amused. "That you are," he says, holding the door for me to pass.

When we're in the hallway and the door closes, I feel lighter, happier, relieved even. I seize the opportunity to tease him. "So, you're a warlock?" I grin.

He stares at me sidelong, narrowing his dark brown eyes. "Sometimes." He shrugs and opens the café's door.

My face contorts in bewilderment. *Sometimes?* What kind of answer is that?

14

LUCIANA

I don't know whether it's Natalya's spell or today's outing with Gavriil, but by the time we return to the house, my mood has greatly improved. Not only am I relieved and less worried, but I'm genuinely happy as I cross the door and move through the hall.

Gavriil walks beside me. Out of the corner of my eye, I see him remove his coat and hang it in the vestibule's closet. "We could dine out," he suggests, "if you'd like."

I turn to face him, and the most brilliant plan occurs to me. "No need," I say. "I have something better in mind."

"Oh?" His attention anchors on me fully.

"I'm fixing dinner for you," I tell him, dropping

my bag on a chair by the fireplace. "Hope you like Italian." I tug away my jacket. The house is warm and cozy. Central heating. Delightful.

Gavriil bites his lower lip. "Sounds good…" he says, the words drift into silence. "But you don't have to do this. I can…"

"I want to," I interrupt him. "It's my way of saying thanks for all you've done for me." My cheeks grow warm. "You and Sasha." I pull back a stray lock of hair behind my ear.

"Actually…" Sasha says. He stands in the doorway. "I'm thinking I might go back to the Pantheon."

Gavriil's eyes brighten. "Really?" he whispers, pleased. "That's a wonderful idea."

"Thanks, Luciana." Sasha gives me a brief smile. "I'm sorry I can't stay."

"That's all right," I tell him. My heart is lighter than it was yesterday and nothing can spoil this feeling. "Have fun." I would have teased him, but I'm not that well acquainted with the man.

Sasha purses his lips. He moves closer to Gavriil and speaks into his ear. I can't listen to a thing, but Gavriil nods, and his semblance does not change. That's a good sign.

I watch Sasha as he leaves. It's just Gavriil and me

now. "I guess I'll go find the kitchen," I mumble, picking at my nails.

Gavriil takes a step towards me, but stops in the middle of the hall. "I can help… if you need me." The softness of his tone and the gentle stare of his dark eyes wash away from me any dregs of anxiety.

Slowly, I come to realize that I'm smiling at him. I'm sure I must be gawking at the man. Ugh… I shake my head. "You know what? Yes. I'd love some help."

Gavriil's taciturn demeanor thaws, giving way to a warmer expression. "I'll show you the way," he says.

15

LUCIANA

I stop at the kitchen's threshold. It's huge. I don't even know where to begin.

Gavriil moves past me, tying his hair into a low coil. He then unbuttons his shirt's sleeves and rolls them up below his elbows. "All right," he says under his breath. Hands cinched to his waist, he sweeps the room with a glance, as though it's the first time he's set foot inside, which might be true. "If I were the chef, where would I keep the pasta?" Long and sturdy fingers smooth across the cabinets. He opens a few with no success.

I do the same. "This kitchen's so big, it should come with a floor plan." I choke a laugh.

He sniggers. "I'm sure there is one," he teases. "Found it."

I open a door and find the pantry. "Me too!" I cheer.

As I'm filling my arms with tomatoes and onions, I come across an even nicer discovery. "A-ha…" I say, reaching for the bottle. "Looks like Chef has a secret love affair with vodka."

"Seriously?" Gavriil frowns. He sneaks up behind me so fast that I startle. I almost fall, but he catches my shoulders and steadies me. And then his brawny arm glides beside me. Gavriil grabs the bottle and reads the label. "Huh…" he says. "Beluga." One eyebrow shoots skyward in astonishment. "Gold Line."

I tilt my head and lean closer to see. "He's got great taste." I shrug. "Come on. Let's take everything to the table."

Gavriil nods. He slips the bottle inside the cabinet.

"No, no…" I all but sing as I head to the kitchen island. "Make sure to bring that too."

He doesn't put up much of a fight and does as I say.

I set the veggies on the table, then grab a knife and start dicing. "We'll need some meat," I mumble.

Gavriil opens the freezer and slips the bottle in there. "*Secondo piatto?*" he says. His Italian accent is charming. Bad, but still charming. He points at the refrigerator.

I stand in front of the white wood panel and pull the handle. At once, I am in awe. The bulk of food inside the fridge seems far too much for two grown men. Beef, veal, venison, lamb... this could well be a butcher's shop. "Whoa..." I utter, baffled. "That's a lot of meat."

Gavriil stares at me, troubled.

"Listen, I only wish my fridge were half as full..." I crack a smile. "Grocery shopping is not my forte." I grab what I need and head back to the table.

Gavriil adds the pasta to the boiling water, and I do my thing, working on the sauce. "So..." I tell him as coolly as I can. "What's the story?"

He starts. "The story?" he asks, creasing his brow.

"Yes," I say, starting the blender. When the noise is over, I add, "Between Natalya and Sasha..." Gavriil takes the blender from my hands and sets it next to the hot pan. "If you can talk about it, that is."

"Oh, *that* story." He almost sounds relieved. "They used to date, long ago," he begins. "They must have been around fifteen, I believe." Gavriil splashes the sauce into the pan. "I honestly thought they'd be matched forever."

"Forever?" I say in disbelief.

"When you know, you know." He shrugs his shoulders.

"But still, fifteen?" I pause. "That's awfully young to make such a commitment..." I strain the pasta in the sink.

Gavriil season's the meat and moves it to the stove. He already has the skillet ready with olive oil, red pepper seeds, garlic, and cooked onions. "Not for my people," he says, both eyebrows shooting sky-high. He sears the meat with such confidence, you'd think he cooks for himself all the time. "Some of them consider me a confirmed bachelor."

I stop everything, intrigued. "How old are you?" I have to ask.

He stirs the sauce, and when he removes the spoon, it drips on his hand. "Twenty-four." Gavriil shrugs, licking the sauce off his thumb. He does it offhandedly, but the gesture itself is impossibly sexy. A thrill shoots through my core and between my legs without remedy.

I swallow hard and force myself to look away. He's so attractive. My mind spins in a daze, swept in a cloud of undiluted fascination and complete idiocy... I don't think I've ever felt this way about anyone.

"And you?" he asks, stirring the pot again. God, he's stirring so much more than that.

"Twenty-three…"

"Oh," he says, impressed. "And you're your own boss?" He sets the spoon aside.

"I have an antique shop…" The words roll out, but I am besotted with that image of him licking his thumb. *Stop it, Luciana!* I shut my eyes for a moment, then force myself to keep my mind busy with something else.

I take over the meat. "Rare, right?" I ask.

"Yeah." He leans against the counter and tosses the kitchen cloth over his shoulder. "An antique shop…" His arms corded in muscle fold over his chest. "That sounds interesting." Gavriil's entire focus is on me, and I do not know how to handle it.

"My grandfather left me the business when he passed away," I say in a blurt. "That, and a bunch of rentals."

When he moves to the sink to wash his hands, the restlessness inside me starts to fade. "He left you well provided," he adds, drying his sturdy arms with the cloth.

"Uh-huh." I bite my lower lip. *Focus on the meat… Not 'that' meat, Luciana.* God, I can't stop blushing. I'll blame it on the stove if I have to. My gaze centers on the skillet.

But my easiness is short-lived when Gavriil's hand

rests next to mine over the counter. He stands inches behind me. I can feel his warm breath caressing my cheek in slow, thrilling waves. His other hand slides the tongs away from my fingers. He turns the steaks, searing them evenly.

I get a whiff of his cologne, tied up with his musky fragrance. He's never been as close to me as he is right now. My heart beats hard against my chest. Every inch of me goes taut at his nearness.

"Beautiful," he purrs in my ear. His husky voice makes my entire body tingle. My cheeks burn like crazy. For a second, I don't think he's talking about the meat... A girl can dream, can't she?

Finally, he steps away. I exhale one long breath. My hand slightly trembles as I lower the burner's temperature. Meanwhile, Gavriil covers the sauce pot and lowers the flame. He sets the timer.

And now, we wait.

I grab a stool by the kitchen island and sit there, leaning my elbows on the counter when a couple of chilled shot glasses slide down the marble slab and stop in front of me. My head swings to Gavriil. A hint of mischief glints in his dark brown eyes. He's ready with the bottle of vodka in his hands.

I take my glass and silently tell him to fill it up. Fierce as a wildcat, he leans over the table, narrowing his eyes. "Are you sure you're ready for this?" he teases. His demeanor is quiet and self-possessed, as usual, but bolder.

I throw him a knowing look, faking all the confidence I'm lacking. "Are *you*?" I tell him.

Gavriil licks his lower lip, delighted. "Is that a challenge?" he says, cracking the clay seal with his bare hand. He pours the drinks.

"Just one for you," he says, handing me my shot glass. *As if.* "*Za vstrechu.*" He raises his drink to eye level. "To our meeting." Gavriil tilts his shot towards me. We clink the glasses and it's magic. I can't understand it, but the air between us suddenly becomes electrifying.

We take the shots. To him, it slips like water down his throat. To me, it burns and I can't help grimacing. I see him watching me. The way he kills the smile already blooming on his silken lips... He pours himself another drink.

"Hey," I whine.

"In Russia, there's no waiting between first and second rounds," he almost sings.

I glare at him. "Well, if you're having another, I want one too. So fill it!" I give him my glass.

It doesn't take much to persuade him. We have

another shot. This one doesn't burn as much. I'm actually enjoying it.

The timer rings. Gavriil turns off the stove. He sets aside the skillet and serves our dishes. "Mm… Sasha would be proud." He drags a stool and sits next to me.

I grab the bottle of Beluga and pour us another shot. *"Salute,"* I say.

A heartfelt smile stretches his lips. It makes my limbs melt. "I know what we need," I say, leaning forward as I hold his warm stare.

Gavriil rests his strong jaw in his fist. "What do we need?" he whispers. His voice is sensual and intimate. His widened pupils swallow me whole... Unstoppable waves of excitement wash over me. I cannot look away.

"Music," I say simply.

He takes out his cell phone and opens an app. "Here." He offers me the phone. "Choose anything you like." His serene maroon eyes find mine again. He stares at me with such intent that it makes my heart turn over in response.

Out of the corner of my eye, I see him fill the glasses. I'm going through his playlists, delighted as I discover that his favorite songs match mine. I choose the one with an ethereal dream-like vibe, and the music plays in the house through a ceiling speaker system.

Gavriil hands me my glass. He makes another toast in Russian. A shock ripples through my body each time he speaks in his mother tongue. I don't think he realizes how attractive he is, even more so now that he's loosened up. I don't even ask him what he said. I simply pour the delicious vodka down my throat and enjoy every single part of this moment.

He lowers his glass and sets it in front of him. He then crosses his arms over the table and hunches a little. A soft sigh sails through his lips. "You continue to amaze me, Luciana..." he blurts.

"Huh?" I pout, pushing my glass aside.

He rakes his fingers through his hair, suppressing a smile. "When I told you that your boyfriend was a vampire..."

"He wasn't my boyfriend." I bristle. God, how many times do I have to say it?

Gavriil shoots me a knowing look. "When I told you," he continues, "you took the news rather well..." He bites his lower lip. "Then I take you to Natalya, and you don't even question the fact that she's a witch." He shrugs matter-of-factly.

My brow furrows. "Why would I?"

"Exactly," he says, baffled, for some reason.

"Then she tells you I'm a warlock," he mumbles with a vacant stare, almost to himself. "You don't even flinch."

A snigger escapes from my mouth. "Is that all you've got?" I taunt him.

His darkened stare cuts to mine. "Oh, I've got more…" His intensity jolts my heart into a quickened beat.

I hold my breath, trying to pace my pulse. But it doesn't do much to help. "Really?" I manage. "Well, let's hear it."

Gavriil heaves a deep sigh. His gaze drifts towards the vodka. "I'm gonna need another one of these first…" he says, grabbing the bottle, then pouring himself a drink.

I push my glass towards him, but he holds it by the rim and puts it away. "No, no…" he groans. "I want you sober for this." Another sharp stare locks in my eyes. "As sober as possible, that is."

I scoff. "I'm perfectly fine," I tell him. The fact that I have to say it makes me giggle. I roll my eyes back. My face feels so warm. "Spill it."

Gavriil drinks the shot. His fingers glide over his lips for a second. "When you asked if I was a vampire hunter," he begins, hesitant, "you weren't all that astray." He swallows hard. "Vampires have natural enemies. You see…"

"You're a warlock," I say in reassurance. "I know."

"I am *more* than that," he says in a low voice.

"Like what?" I blurt. "A werewolf?" A smile thins my lips.

His expression remains impassive. "Try another beast," he murmurs, looking away. "Like… a bear."

Shock flies through me. "What?"

"Yeah…"

I am too stunned to weave sounds into words. However, I push through my tied tongue. "You're a… shapeshifter?" I manage with a broken voice.

"Yeah," he exhales. Still no eye contact.

"But, how?" I mumble, bemused. Words wedge in my throat. "I've never seen… Can you control it?" Finally, I say something sensible.

"Usually, yeah."

Usually? Now I begin to panic. Sheer black fright washes over me. "Am I in danger…" I barely speak the words, "from you?"

His fierce gaze angles to me, a hand seizing my wrist fast. "Never," he whispers, earnest in his tone. "You have *nothing* to fear from me, Luciana. I promise you." His fingers burn into my skin.

I'm instantly awake. Every ounce of alcohol has

evaporated from my system. "Is this a *full moon* kind of thing?" I hear myself say, clumsily.

"No," he assures me with the sweetest disposition. "It's a *mad-as-hell* kind of thing." Gavriil pauses. "Like *really* mad. *Fight or flight* mad."

"Okay," I breathe. He still hasn't let me go. And the worst part is, I don't want him to. "Okay..." I swallow again. My throat is dry as hell. "I'm gonna need that shot now."

He nods, stern in his expression. Swiftly, he fills my glass. My hands quiver when I take it. I don't know if it's his nearness or the news that makes me rattle inside and out. Maybe it's both.

"So, your friends..." My voice drifts into a hushed whisper. "The ones you called in. They are..."

"My brothers," Gavriil adds, and his voice is smooth and soothing. "Yes, they're bear shifters as well." He pauses. "They've been guarding us for a while now. They won't let any vampires get close to you."

"Why would they do that?" I snap as it sinks in. "Why would they risk their lives for a complete stranger?"

"Because..." he says, pouring himself a drink, "I asked them to."

I scowl. "But why would they listen to you?" I add. "You're…"

"Their king." The words sail through his lips. He immediately covers his mouth with his fingers. I'm assuming he wasn't supposed to say it.

A chill drops down my spine. "You're…" I can't even say it. I shake my head. "You're the king of the…?"

"Ursa Clan," he adds.

I look at him with surprise. "Is there anything else, Gavriil?" I say cautiously. "*Anything* more shocking than this that I should know about?"

"Nope," he manages. "That's pretty much it."

"*Bene…*" I slowly nod, then suck in one long breath. How can I even begin to fit all this in my head?

He clears his throat, pushing back the stool. "This is too much for you," he decides. "I should go. My presence will do nothing but disturb you…"

I grab his wrist before he can slide his hand off the table. "Please don't do this," I say in a low voice.

He stares at me, perplexed.

"Don't decide for me how I feel or what I think," I add.

His expression slips from bemusement into something more subdued that resembles pain.

"Luciana…" he begs, tilting his head. "You don't have to…"

I rise from the seat. "I don't *have* to do anything," I tell him. It comes out harsher than I would have wanted, but there it is. "I don't have to stay here, and I do. I don't have to cook dinner with you, and I do." A pause. "I do these things because I want to, Gavriil." One scant breath. "I don't *have* to like you, and I do… because I want to."

His eyes darken with emotion. Gavriil's lips part, but no sound comes through.

I glide my hand away from him, painful as it is to let him go. "So," I add, finishing my shot's dregs. "Let's eat."

He quietly nods, rising from the seat to serve our dishes. And thank goodness for that, because I'm starting to feel woozy. When he comes back, he slides the steaming plate before me.

"This looks delicious." I grab my fork. All the while, I'm trying not to think too much about Gavriil's shocking revelation. I try not to make my astonishment so damn obvious. If I can wrap my head around Trent being a vampire, I can sure as hell understand Gavriil is a shapeshifter.

I wish I could find a way to hold a casual conversation with him. But I can't. So many questions whirl in my mind, it's impossible not to speak them. Finally, I start with, "Can I ask you…?"

"You may ask anything," he interrupts in an earnest tone.

I twist the fork in the pasta, careful not to meet his striking maroon eyes. My frail courage might vanish if I do. "How long have you been…?" the words drift into silence. I give up and look at him.

"A shapeshifter?" he says, his full attention narrowed on me. He could not care less there's a fragrant meal set before him.

"Yeah…" Good grief, now I'm stealing his *yeahs*. I look down at the table. When I look at him again, a stray lock of hair covers my face.

Gavriil leans closer. His firm hand takes the strands and carefully pushes them behind my ear. Shivers shoot through my limbs. "It's been in my blood for generations," he says with a quiet voice, still focused on me. "The beast manifests at sixteen… I was seventeen when I became the clan's king."

"That seems pretty young," I blurt.

"So were you when you claimed your inheritance," he counters, stating a fact.

I blush immediately. "Yes, but… that was different." I set the fork down. "My grandfather left me an accountant, lawyers, and a trust…"

"My father took the same precautions," he says. "He surrounded me with loyal advisors and a royal guard."

I stare at him. It's not what he says, but what he doesn't speak that gets me. In silence, he's saying to me: *We're not that different.* And I guess that's true—except for the magical part.

"A vampire killed him," he adds in a bitter tone that makes me shudder. Gavriil picks up the knife and carves into his steak. I glimpse the pink meat as the slice drops on the plate... A bear shifter. No wonder he likes his meat raw.

"I'm sorry," I whisper.

"It was a long time ago. That vampire's dead now," he assures me, pensive while he stares at his dish. "You should eat something before all that vodka *really* kicks in." A subtle smirk curls the corner of his lips.

He's right. I pick up my fork and dig into the pasta.

"I'm going to take down the head vampire in the city," he says offhandedly, carving another slice of meat. "Nobody will come close to you then."

I stare at him with shuddering eyes. "Gavriil..." I whisper. He just spoke of his dead father and the fiend that killed him. I could all but touch the pain as it poured through his words, and he simply drops the subject like it's nothing.

"I'll hold a meeting with my Elite guard tomorrow," he continues. "Sasha tells me they've come up with a plan." He chews his meat and swallows.

A shiver scurries through me as I see him raise this fence of ice around him.

He sighs with weariness. "The sooner we deal with him, the quicker you can go back to your normal life."

It hurts, this sudden change in him. I can't understand it. A moment ago, he just bared his soul to me. And now this? God, I just told him I liked him, and now he wants me out of his life? "I'm not in a hurry," I almost mutter, locking eyes with him. "Are you?"

Gavriil drops the fork and knife and pushes his dish away with his forearm. He sweeps a hand across his forehead. "It's late," he says, rising from the seat. "We should get some sleep." He picks up the dish and leaves it in the sink.

Seriously? I want to grab him by the shoulders and shake some sense into him. But I've already put myself out there enough. I'm not going to beg. He wants to leave? Fine.

I grab my dish and do the same.

16

GAVRIIL

I'm standing on the library's terrace, trying to fill my mind with anything other than Luciana's hazel eyes. I even texted Sasha, but he's not yet replied, and I don't think he will for a while. Maybe I should follow my own rotten advice and go to bed. But what good would that do? I won't sleep. I can't stop thinking about her.

Even as my bear lays dormant, I feel a relentless pull towards her. She makes every moment memorable. Being with Luciana is always easy, so much so, that I opened myself to her in that kitchen as I've never done before with anyone—not even Bella.

She *likes* me. She just admitted to it hours ago, and all I could do was tell her I'd get out of her life as soon as possible... My world is as screwed up as it gets. I don't want her to get hurt.

Fuck. The last thing I want is to ruin this, and I think I have already. A low growl lingers in my chest. "Where's that vodka?" I groan, heading back to the kitchen.

Without the staff and the usual guests, the house is silent and still. I meander in the twilight, sweeping up my hair and tying it in a quick bun. I unfasten the top buttons of my shirt.

Bottle in hand, I walk into the living room, careful not to make a sound. It's around midnight, and Luciana is sleeping. At least one of us gets to have a good night's rest.

I grab a log and start a fire. How did my life get so complicated? I was supposed to be here on a holiday. The first, after almost a decade of leading the Ursa Clan. Instead, I get in trouble with the Roman vampire coven... *See, this is why I seldom travel.* I gasp and open the bottle. Oh, I'll make them pay.

"Shouldn't you be sleeping?" she says.

I jerk back in a flash, heart shocked into a wild gallop. She's sitting on the couch in the darkness. There's something in her hands... a tub of ice cream. She's wearing that oversized t-shirt, hair pinned up in a messy updo. Gods, I didn't pick up her presence. Natalya's spells are that powerful.

"What are you doing here?" I blurt. My mouth goes dry in an instant.

"I couldn't sleep," we say in unison.

"You were in such a hurry to go to bed, I figured…" she mumbles, putting the lid on the tub.

"Luciana." Subdued, I go to meet her. "I'm sorry about that."

"Mm…" She puts away the tub of ice cream. Her eyes shimmer with sadness.

I sit beside her, fighting the impulse to pull her to me. However, I lean closer. "I did not mean to hurt you," I say in a soft tone. "The truth is… I like you… a lot." My hand cups the side of her face. Gently, I stroke her cheek with my thumb.

"Then, what's the problem?" she whispers, wounded.

"Your world and mine," I explain. "You're in grave danger as it is. Being with me would only worsen matters for you. I have…" the words break, "so many enemies." The air in my throat freezes, but I push through it. "I won't risk your life like that."

"Isn't that my choice to make?" she breathes.

The warmth of tears gathers in my eyes. I look away and nod slowly.

She inches closer until we share the same breathing space. Her delicate hands smooth over my strong jawline and pull me to her. "Then let me," she whispers, bringing her mouth close to mine. She kisses me, lingering, savoring every moment. The touch of her lips delivers a shock wave through my body. I return her kiss with the same sweetness, gradually becoming free of all my worries. Until there's only her and me, and the warmth of her, the maddening presence of her, enclosing me in the purest bliss.

My fingers glide through her blonde hair until the heavy locks cascade below her shoulders. The tenderness of her kiss soon dissolves and gives way to wild intensity. A low moan escapes me when her tongue teases my lips apart. "Luciana," I speak against her sensual lips. As her kiss becomes more demanding, my hunger for her rises.

"Luciana…" I beg, forced to resist the torture of her lips.

"It's all right," she whispers, gliding over my lap, straddling me with her smooth thighs.

Gods, I want her. Desire burns through me in overpowering waves. It would be easy for me to ravish her right now, to have my way as I've wanted ever since I caught her scent. The bear in me roars, demanding, but I silence it fast. "We don't have to do this now," I purr in her ear, unable to stop myself from licking her earlobe and nipping it with my teeth.

With both hands pressed against my chest, she pulls back. Our gazes lock in a powerful stare. "A horde of vampires might kill me at any moment," she says, eyes glistening with desire. "I'm not putting this off."

Lust, fierce and violent, takes over me. I seize her waist and neck and pull her to me, harshly. I claim her mouth in a passionate kiss, delighted as her fingers glide over my shirt, unbuttoning it fast until the warm air hits my chest. Every certainty I've ever had fades away, replaced by the firm conviction that my sole purpose is to please her and grant her every whim.

On an impulse of passion, I raise her hips and lay her on the couch, where she lies panting, waiting for my next move. My gaze roves over her sensual figure, her beautiful blushing face, her full lips reddened by my kisses. Like an untamed beast, I stoop over her, smoothing my hands over her thighs. My heart pumps harder and faster. I'm ready to unveil her and discover her naked body for the first time. And as my hands reach the rim of her t-shirt, the doorbell rings.

17

LUCIANA

A growl rumbles in Gavriil's throat. His fierce gaze angles to the hall, but I seize his jaw and pull him back to me, reclaiming his lips in a savage kiss. Every inch of me wants him. I won't hold back another minute. And this man, this wonderful shape-shifting man who has unlocked me, body and soul, is suddenly distracted by the doorbell.

"Forget about that," I beg, crushing my lips against his.

Hesitation looms in his eyes only for an instant. And I read the struggle between bear and man. One of them wins, and his taut body lands over mine. Gavriil's panting breaths shoot lightning through my core, an unstoppable thrill that makes me crave him with insane hunger. His fist closes in my hair and pulls slightly while his mouth devours me with sultry kisses. And I want more of him. I want to be full of him, to have him completely.

Again, the doorbell rings.

This time, we ignore it. Gavriil sinks his knees between mine, forcing apart my legs. "Yes..." I moan. My heart throbs in my ears. My fingers are numb and I can barely breathe, wrapped in a whirlwind of desire.

"Luciana!" a voice calls from the street. "Open up! I know she's in there!"

Gavriil reluctantly parts from me. He stares at the hallway, brow furrowed in undiluted fury.

"Crap," I say under my panting breath. Shock washes over me as every part of my body still tingles.

"Luciana!" the man outside insists.

Gavriil locks eyes with me, perplexed.

I gasp. "It's my friend, Marco..." I facepalm myself.

His maroon eyes show the wounded dullness of disbelief.

"I should..." I mumble, pointing at the hallway. "I should get the door." Slowly, I glide underneath him. This is so embarrassing. But I know if I don't get that, Marco will probably do something crazy, like break inside.

I look back and see Gavriil sitting on the couch, breathless and impossibly gorgeous. Marco could not have appeared at a worse time... And how the hell did he find me?

The hall's marble floor is cold under my bare feet. "Jesus!" I tiptoe to the door and press the buzzer. "Marco..." I manage, then open the gates.

When he stands on the front porch, I open the door. My friend's face slackens. "Luciana, are you hurt?" He steps inside and wanders to the middle of the hall, sweeping it with a glance. "What are you doing here?" Marco turns to me. "You never answered my calls. I was so worried!" Now he's angry.

I purse my lips. "I've... been... busy."

He looks over my shoulder. "Yes, I can see that..." he mumbles.

I turn. Gavriil is standing at the living room doorway, hands in his pants pockets, shoulders squared. He's perfectly strong and impassive as he leans against the door's jamb. One look at his chiseled abs through the disheveled shirt is enough to make me blush again. Gavriil doesn't have a six-pack, but eight muscles that lead to an expanse of taut flesh... He stares at us from a distance, alert yet granting me the space to deal with this myself.

When I face Marco again, he glares at me harshly,

disapproving. His green eyes are about to pop out of their sockets.

I return his stare with a glower of my own, silently saying, *Mind your own business!* My face is burning. "How did you find me?" I tell him in the calmest voice possible.

"I have you on that app, remember?" Marco snaps. "The Friends one?"

"Oh… yeah." I frown.

Marco takes a hand to his waist. "At first, I was like, *This thing isn't working, she lives across the street…*" His gaze drifts to Gavriil again. "I totally get it now."

My eyes widen in shock. "God, Marco!" I all but hiss through clenched teeth. "Thanks for checking on me. I'm fine... Is there anything else?"

He flinches. "You mean other than waiting for you to explain to me how all this happened?" He shoots a groomed eyebrow skyward. "No. Other than that, everything's peachy."

Marco is adorable and obnoxious as an older brother would be.

"We can talk about this later," I say, grabbing his arm, all but dragging him towards the door. "I promise."

His tigerish eyes narrow, still looking towards the

living room, even though I'm sure he can't see Gavriil anymore. "Trent was handsome and all," Marco mumbles. "But this one… He's definitely an upgrade, Luce." He bites his lower lip. "Does he have a friend? A brother, maybe?" Now he's just teasing me.

If I peel my eyes any wider, I'm sure they'll fall off. "I'll talk to you soon," I assure him, opening the door. "Thank you for coming, Marco. I mean it."

He snickers. "All right, woman. I get it," he blurts, crossing the threshold. "Just, please. Check your phone, okay?"

"I will, Marco." I give him a slight smile.

Marco chokes a laugh. *"Bene, bene…"* He grins in absolute mischief. *"Va bene, cara."* His hand glides over my jawline. He pulls me to him and kisses my cheek.

Marco Pellegrini

18

GAVRIIL

ho is that guy, Marco? Why does he kiss her? He's obviously not a threat to Luciana. Otherwise, my brothers would have stopped him. Still, I'm happy he's leaving. She's closing the door. What's going to happen now? Has she changed her mind, maybe?

A soft gasp sails through my lips.

My sanity is pending from the frailest thread as I stand in the doorway. I don't want to pressure her. Whatever she chooses is fine. Even though I'm already fired up, aching for her touch.

She slowly turns around. Luciana leaves the hall, tiptoeing through the cold marble checkerboard floors. My heart thumps hard against my chest. I have little to no control over my rapid breaths as I lay eyes on her, so sexy in her white t-shirt.

Luciana stops at the hallway. Our stares lock, and I swallow hard when suddenly she runs to me, mischief tugging at her lips. I can't help but smile, elated, as she jumps to my arms, clasping her hands around my neck. I grab her hips and lift her off the ground, pleasantly surprised as her mouth seals mine in the deepest kiss.

"D'you want this?" I mumble against her lips, kissing her with a maddening, joyous frenzy.

Her fingers glide through my hair. She parts from me but an inch, gleaming hazel eyes full of blissful desire. "I want *you*," she tells me, and she speaks each word with careful intent. "*All of you. The man, the bear, the warlock.*"

My heart is going to explode in my chest. Unable to stop from smiling, I carry her, weightless, in my arms, and take her to my bedroom.

19

GAVRIIL

A delightful shiver of wanting runs through me as we strip each other's clothes. My skin aches for her touch, aches for that contact, flesh on flesh. Still, my gaze roves over her, breathless as I contemplate the passionate beauty of her naked body. Luciana lies on the bed, hazel eyes glazed with desire, cheeks and lips flushed with excitement. The beast inside me claims for immediacy to satisfy its violent desires, but I tame it fast and silence its growls in an instant.

I want to take my time discovering her, learning her by heart, until I know what makes her thrill beneath my fingers. Every inch of me goes taut the moment I press her against my chest, smoothing a hand on her jawline, pulling her to me gently until our lips touch in one slow, sensuous kiss. "We're gonna take this as far as you want," I whisper against her mouth.

She nods. Driven by her own desire, her every curve molds to the firm planes of my body.

I ease her back on the bed and explore her, searing a trail of kisses down her neck to the delicate pit of her collarbone. Her heart throbs hard against my ear when I take my lips lower, to the marble hardness of her nipple. A low moan sails through her lips. She trembles with excitement. And as her passion rises, mine burns wilder.

My hand smooths down her silken belly, finding the way to the place of her pleasure. In an instant, her body arches at the lightness of my teasing touch. I take my kiss there and let it linger lazily. Her quiet moans and panting breaths become my guide, until her body convulses in a rush of ecstasy, followed by another, and another after that.

I scent the purest delight flowing through her. With panting breath, I find her mouth with an unhurried kiss that she returns with reckless abandon. "D'you want more?" I whisper. Between each word, I kiss her cheeks, her neck, her shoulder.

"Uh-huh," she moans, seizing my jawline, taking me back to her mouth.

A flash of ecstasy, her tongue sliding between my lips. Waves of desire crash into my core, begging for release. "What do you want?" I purr, restraining the demands that burn inside me.

"I want you," she says, twisting her expression as she stiffens, taken by merciless hunger.

"D'you want me inside of you?" I breathe while my hand sears a path from her abdomen to her silky thigh.

"God, yes…" she mumbles, biting her lower lip, and my heartbeat rides into a wild gallop.

Gently, I push a stray lock of hair away from her face and wait until her eyes open. And when they do, I take her quivering hand to me, her touch unleashing a thrill that electrifies my limbs. Led by Luciana, my body lowers over hers. I gasp in sweet agony as she welcomes me into her. My body blends against her, and in an instant, she becomes everything to me—the moon and stars, the air I breathe, the warm blood that pumps hard and fast inside my veins.

In a fit of passion, I grab her hips and pull her to me, roughly. Our bodies rock together in flawless harmony, soaring higher and higher until we almost reach the peak of delight. I smooth my hands up her waist, sweeping the curves of her breasts, until my palms set on the sides of her face. "Luciana," I say in a ragged whisper. "Open your eyes."

Drunken desire fills her hazel eyes when they lock on mine. "Come with me," I tell her.

"Oh God… Gavriil!" she moans as waves of ecstasy ripple through her body, casting echoes in my own. I cry her name, longing for release. And together, we shatter into a million gleaming stars.

My bear reacts, taken by the tide of fathomless pleasure, and I feel my fangs drop, ready to cast a bite on Luciana's bare shoulder. I draw my lips closer. One bite and she'll be mine forever.

I want to claim her, to brand her as my own, and call her *mine* from this night onward. "Yes," I gasp, inching closer, when suddenly I growl and turn my face away fast. My breathing races even more. My body shudders as fright and ecstasy collide inside me.

I can't do it. I shouldn't.

I claw at the mattress, looking away from her, burdened by shame.

"Gavriil?" Luciana's voice is sweet as honey as she crawls to me, delicate fingers gliding through my hair.

Passion pounds through my blood still. Tainted with dread.

"What is it?" she presses in a low whisper.

"Forgive me," I say between quick breaths.

She cradles my head and brings me to her, and I yield to her demand, subdued. "There is nothing to forgive," she whispers, concerned. "What's wrong?"

"The bear in me," I manage, avoiding her earnest stare. "It wants you…" my voice breaks. "It's wanted you for a while now."

"I see nothing wrong with that," she says, consoling my wretchedness.

My gaze cuts to hers. "You don't understand," I tell her. "If I claim you now, there's no going back."

Bemusement surfaces on her face. "Gavriil, I…" she whispers. Her delicate hand glides over my jawline as she tilts her head.

I love you, I want to tell her. *I love you with such violence that it frightens me.* Instead, I crush her to me, capturing her mouth with mine. Then I hold her in my arms, tightly. My stare shoots skywards as tears rim my eyes. Gods, my feelings for her are stronger than I ever imagined. I was only able to stop myself now because of Natalya's spell. Had Luciana's scent not been veiled by magic, tonight might've gone horribly wrong.

LUCIANA

I take one deep breath as I wake the next morning. Instantly, I pick up Gavriil's fragrance, permeating my skin. When my eyes open, I find him lying next to me, glistening in the morning light as it spills over his taut and muscular body.

Being with him was the closest thing to magic I have ever experienced. A thrill rushes through me as I remember how he shed from his usual dispassionate nature and transformed into the most fierce and giving lover. Suddenly, I crave him again. I snuggle against his chest, waiting for him to wake up. I'm reminded of that last thing he said. *If I claim you, there's no going back.* What is that supposed to mean?

His firm hand glides to my waist, long fingers lingering on my hips, pulling me to him. I turn and meet his dark brown eyes, delighted by the subtle smile that tugs the corner of his lips. "Good morning," he purrs, watching me with lazy longing.

God, it's like a dream, waking up to this gorgeous man. *"Buongiorno, bello…" Good morning, handsome,* I mumble, pressing my lips against his shoulder. Is he blushing? He is.

A dimple pierces his cheek as he grins. He seizes my hips and rolls me on top of him until we share breath. I sense him ready for another round of passion, and I long for it too. But my mind whirls with the incessant question, and I need an answer.

"You and I have to talk," I tell him. Immediately, I bite my lower lip, regretting the words a little.

The light in Gavriil's countenance slowly fades. "Oh…?"

"Yeah," I whisper, half in anticipation, half in dread. "About last night. You said…"

His phone rings. Gavriil swings his head to the night table. He stares at the screen and reads the word SASHA. "I should… get that," he mumbles.

I nod, reluctantly.

He grabs the phone and glides to the edge of the bed. "Yeah…" he groans. "When?" He sits on the bed fast. "Get everyone here. NOW." He hangs up, then grabs his boxer shorts from the floor and slips them on. Still sitting on the bed, Gavriil sighs, rubbing a hand across his brow.

A tense silence spreads in the room. And I break it. "What's wrong?" I say, sitting on the bed. I crush the sheets against my bare chest, fearful of the answer.

He looks over his bare shoulder, pursing his lips. After a moment, he turns to me and cups the side of my face, concern twisting his expression. "Luciana," he whispers, dark maroon eyes locked on mine. "I need you to be strong."

I gasp, realizing a shiver of panic. "Tell me," I breathe.

"They have him," he says all too quickly. "Your friend, Marco. The coven has him."

Sheer dread washes over me. I can't breathe. I can't speak. Gavriil holds me in a firm embrace. Tears blur my vision. I don't even know what to say. Quiet sobs escape my lips, and he presses me to him.

"We're gonna get him back," he says in a low, soothing voice. "It's gonna be all right."

I nod as tears glide down my cheeks. I want to believe him. Never has this felt so real.

"I'm meeting my brothers in a moment," he speaks in my ear, stroking the side of my face with his temple. "Please wait for me here." His sensual lips press against my forehead.

"No," I manage, hurting.

He frowns.

I push back until our stares meet. "If you're gonna talk about Marco with them, I want to be there," I add.

"Luciana…"

I clear my tears with the back of my hand. "I'm going," I breathe. "Nothing you can say will change my mind."

A low growl lingers in his chest. His gaze drifts from me for a minute. And then, he silently agrees.

21

GAVRIIL

We gather in the parlor. I stand in the middle of the room, surrounded by my brothers. The air is tense. Our hatred towards vampires is nothing new; but when one of us is personally attacked by them, then it's the same as if they'd injured us all. Unity and brotherhood are what make the Ursa Clan strong, and what has guaranteed its endurance across the centuries.

A dozen men, each one the leader of a distinct bear shifter family. Behind each of them, there's at least a squad of twenty of our brothers. More than enough to beat Andrea Barone and his coven of blood drinkers.

"Three hundred?" I ask Sasha in his ear.

He leans towards me. "Five fifty," he replies. "When our brothers in Saint Petersburg learned of our *situation*, they came."

"Do you have a plan?" I say. As my Enforcer, Sasha is the head of any strategy.

He purses his lips and nods.

"Gavriil," someone says. I recognize the voice and it stuns me.

When my head swings to the side, Vladimir Volkov approaches me, fierce silvery eyes fixed on mine.

I start, transfixed. We haven't seen each other in years. "Volodya…" I mumble, too shocked to say anything else. "I didn't expect to see *you* here." *This is an Ursa matter. What business do wolf shifters have in all this?* I want to tell him, but he understands my astonishment.

Volodya pats my arm, a subtle smirk tugging the corner of his lips. "I came as soon as I heard," he says with a stern expression. "My pack is ready to rip some vampire throats whenever you need us."

I read through his countenance and discover the offer is genuine. After all this time, Vlad remains loyal to the clan. Pleased, I glide my hand on his jawline and give him half a smile. "Brother," I say, pulling him towards me. We embrace after seven years of separation. Seeing him is like having a piece of my father with me. He cared dearly for Volodya, took him in at a very young age, when he became an orphan, before I was born. My father raised him as his own.

Slowly, Volodya slips away from my arms, widened eyes fixed on the parlor's entrance. He steps back. I see his breathing race, his pitch-black pupils widen until there's but a rim of silver left. In a flash, the scent floods my lungs. The blood chills in my veins. And when Vladimir's countenance turns feral, I have to look back.

Luciana stands in the doorway, radiant in casual ripped jeans and a t-shirt. Long, damp hair ripples over her shoulders. Damp hair... *Fuck. She took a shower.*

One quick glance at the room and I recognize unmistakable restraint in my brothers' gazes. They pick up her scent as well. At this point, she's in as much danger from any of my clan as from the vampires themselves.

Fuck.

I dash to the doorway, grab her arm, and pull her back, closing the doors behind us. Not that it makes much of a difference.

The minute we put a good distance between us

and the room, I stop. "Luciana, are you out of your mind?!" I all but hiss, pulse throbbing hard against my ears and in my throat. I take her hand and lead her as far away from the room as possible.

Bemusement fills her radiant visage with the same intensity as lust washes over me at the powerful perfume of her skin. "What is it?" She frowns. "I don't..."

"Do you realize that room is full of shifters?" I growl, impatient as the bear in me bristles, demanding that I claim her before any of my brothers dares to do it. Fighting my beast with every step, I move upstairs with her. "I've not branded you! I've not claimed you! They could... They..." I can't even say it, struggling between dread and feral desire.

Her eyes widen. "Is it my scent?" she asks, shuddering. "Can they pick up my scent, the same as vampires?" Luciana covers her mouth, panic swelling inside her.

We stop at her bedroom's door. I exhale a long breath. "You need to spray on Natalya's perfume," I urge, for her sake, more than my own. I close my eyes. "*Please.*" My voice comes out strained. Reluctantly, I step away from her.

"You feel it too?" she asks in the sweetest tone.

I close my eyes again, holding my breath this time, hoping it might help. But it does not. "That's how I first found you," I confess. "Now, *please...*"

The blood drains from her face. She darts into the room. I hear the clank of crystal as she goes through the bathroom bottles until that first swish of spray comes through. And only then I breathe, relieved.

I lean my back against the door's jamb and heave a deep sigh. I take one long inhalation and release the air slowly. Her scent still lingers in the air, but it's not as strong... *Fuck. That was close.*

"I didn't know," she whispers, standing in the bathroom's threshold, fearful.

I immediately hate myself for putting her through this. But there was no other way to get her out of that room. There's so much I need to tell her... so much she should know. "Luciana, I'm sorry," I manage. "I am to blame. I should have told you..."

"Is it a bad thing?" she asks, recoiling in the doorway. Her lower lip slightly quivers.

"No..." I assure her in a soothing voice. "No, it's not a bad thing." I take a step inside her room, but when she flinches, my heart shatters.

"It worked," I say, holding my hand up in reassurance. "Your scent is covered now."

"What would you do to me if I were not wearing Natalya's perfume?" she asks in a low-pitched tone, hugging her arms.

I take a step closer. Then another until she lets me hold her hand. "I would have loved you the same way as I loved you last night…" I whisper, leading her to the bed where we then sit. "The bear in me would have branded you, and claimed you mine."

"Branded me? I don't understand what that means," she says, troubled.

I sigh. I've tried to avoid this conversation, telling myself it's too soon. But I guess I can no longer postpone it. Not when the clan gathers downstairs, with the addition of *Vlad-fucking-wolf-shifter*.

My fingers interlace with hers. "When a bear chooses its mate, it claims her forever." A pause. "This can happen in several ways. The most common is through the mating bite." I purse my lips, watching her intently.

"Last night you…" Her words drift into silence, "you wanted to *bite* me?" A subtle frown creases her brow.

I slightly nod.

Her eyes turn wild with bewilderment.

"I know," I whisper, tightening my hold.

"What happens then?" she asks, settling into this new reality.

I lick my lower lip. "I claim you mine," I breathe. "And everyone in my clan knows not to come after you. And any other shifter as well."

The frown furrows deeper in her face. "Then, downstairs, when I…"

"Yeah," I tell her, releasing a gasp of relief immediately afterwards. "There's something in your scent. Something that is too compelling for any of my shifter brothers."

"And vampires," she adds, not particularly thrilled.

"Yeah…" I concede, shrugging my shoulders.

Something clicks in her then. Her gaze cuts to mine. "But last night, I was wearing Natalya's perfume and…"

I glide a hand over her jawline, giving her the hint of a smile. "That was all you," I purr. "Not your scent." Gods, even as the lingering fragrance of her vanishes, I lust for her the same.

Luciana's gaze angles downwards. Her cheeks burn red scarlet. I lean forward. My lips meet hers in one slow kiss. She kisses me back with the same tenderness, then slowly parts from me. "D'you think I can go down now?" She bites her lower lip. "I really want to be there. I want to know how we're gonna help Marco."

"*We?*" I frown. "You're not going anywhere, Luciana. I want you to stay here, where it's safe. I don't want you out there, putting your life at risk…"

"No, Gavriil."

I start. "What?" I exhale. "What do you mean, *no?*" No one has ever said *no* to me. No one who's lived to tell the tale, at least.

"Marco is my friend," she says, smoothing her hand on my arm. "I'm going to do everything I can to save him from those vampires."

I purse my lips. She doesn't even begin to comprehend the vileness of these blood drinkers. I cannot bring myself to tell her that their viciousness knows no limits, that her friend Marco might be dead even as we speak.

No. I cannot crush her like that.

"I don't want to lose you…" For the first time in my life, I hear myself beg.

"And I understand that," she says in the sweetest tone. "But I'm going anyway." Determination hangs from each word. She will not be persuaded. My heart breaks a little at her refusal. No one ever denies me. This is a terrible first. And I don't know how to handle it.

Luciana rises from the bed. "Let's go to this meeting," she says, offering me her hand.

I take it, reluctantly, and follow her. And then, it hits me.

Outside the bedroom, *she's* the fucking alpha.

Vladimir
Volkov

22

LUCIANA

They move the meeting to the courtyard, where the air is *fresher*—meaning *not* permeated with my scent. It's awkward at first having all those stares on me, the only human in the bunch, and a woman. But I don't care. All I can think about is Marco. Each time his face comes to me, I blame myself for not answering his calls. None of this would have happened had I texted him back, telling him I was fine. But I got swept away into a world of vampires and shifters, and gorgeous Gavriil.

This is completely my fault, and I have to fix it.

They all look pretty normal to me. Handsome, powerful men. Even the ones garbed more casually look like they were taken out of a model agency, with taut muscular bodies, chiseled features, and fierce eyes.

"We need to get Andrea out of his lair," the man with stormy eyes says. Gavriil told me he's a wolf shifter and his brother. "We need a distraction, something to steal Andrea's focus. And while he's engaged, we strike at the heart of his lair and rescue the human." When he smirks, I glimpse the fangs. That's all that jumps out of normality. They're a bit longer, and pointier than regular canines. His harsh gaze lingers on me from time to time, always long enough to make me uncomfortable. He's got a secretive smile, like he knows something I do not.

"Bait?" Gavriil mutters. "No offense, brother. But you've been out of the clan for nearly a decade, and suddenly *you're* calling the shots?" A low growl lingers in his chest.

Vlad startles. "Brother, I would never," he says, a cautious hand raised in the air. "I've been living in Rome for three years, and I can tell you, this is what I know of Andrea: he's a sucker for routine. Getting him out of his lair will not be easy. Only the strongest bait will achieve that."

"I don't know of anything that can tempt him," Gavriil says under his breath, straightening his back, opening his chest as he faces Vladimir.

"I do," a voice says in the crowd.

All heads turn to meet the blond shifter with ice-blue eyes. *Sasha.*

Sasha's gaze locks on me.

Gavriil's face slackens when he understands his meaning. "Sasha…" he says through clenched teeth.

"She's the only one who can lure him out," he adds. "Only Luciana can—!"

"Aleksandr!" Gavriil roars, chest heaving, blood rushing to his face. He sucks in one long breath to tame his temper. "That is enough. It's out of the question. There must be another way."

The wolf pierces me with hunter eyes. He speaks to me silently. *"It's your fault this has happened,"* he says. *"Playing along is the least you can do."* His voice is deep and resonant in my head. Gooseflesh shoots up my arms. How the hell is he doing this?

No matter how he's doing it, I hate that he's right. And didn't I tell Gavriil I would do everything I could to get Marco back?

"I'll do it," I say in a blurt, becoming the cynosure of all eyes. My heart is hammering in my chest. My mouth dries in an instant.

Gavriil's face pales. "Luciana," he whispers in my ear, gliding a hand over my bare arm. His touch is persuasive and sensual, but I will not yield.

I push myself to speak again. "Just tell me what to do, and I'll do it."

Gavriil's hold tightens. When I look at him, his gaze is stern and overpowering. "I have to do this," I whisper to him. "Otherwise, Marco will be doomed, and I'll never be free of them."

If I could read his mind, I know what it would say. *I don't want to lose you.* But I have no other choice. And he knows I won't back down, even if he is the Ursa King.

Gavriil's expression gradually softens, and his subdued stare does not stray from my face. "Very well," he says under his breath.

He then turns to his brother, Vlad. "You've obviously given it some thought," he breathes. "What's the plan?"

Vladimir's eyes brighten at the sound of the words. He raises his chin, a subtle smirk quirking his lips. "There's an art gala this weekend," he begins.

"Where?" Gavriil says with impatience.

"Terrazza del Pincio," Vlad replies fast. "If we make it known that you'll be there, I'm sure Andrea will not be able to resist. It's quite an exclusive event… I can get an invita—"

"I'm sure I can get our invitations," Gavriil cuts him off.

Vlad bristles, clenching his jaw, but he regains composure fast. "While both of you attend the gala, along with the Elite of our brethren," he adds, glancing at the group, "I will take my pack to Andrea's lair and strike there." He pauses. "I save the human. You kill Andrea. Everyone's happy."

"Sounds like a good plan," Gavriil says. "Andrea will bring his best blood drinkers with him. You'll be able to rescue the human with little resistance… Sasha, set up the details with the clan."

Sasha silently agrees.

I'm not sure I trust Vlad. There's something about the wolf that makes me shudder. However, Gavriil yields to Vladimir's embrace as the meeting draws to an end. And as the wolf wraps him in his arms, his feral stare angles towards me, roving my face lazily until Bear and Wolf part again.

23

GAVRIIL

When the last of my clan leaves the manor, it's only Vlad and me, standing on the terrace. Even when I am overjoyed to see my brother again, I cannot help harsh resentment from tainting my happiness.

"You came," I mumble, pressing him to speak.

His stormy eyes cut to mine, glistening with magic and earnest sincerity. "How could I not?" he says. "You will always have my support, Gavriil… and my pack's."

"You're living here, in Rome?" I ask, unwavering in my caution.

He nods. "For now," he says under his breath. "You know me… I'm always on the move."

"It was not always so." I raise my brow.

Vlad fixes his cufflinks, struggling to conceal his restlessness. He will not speak of the reasons that led to his estrangement. Perhaps someday he will. I choose not to pressure him.

My gaze drifts to the courtyard, where Luciana wanders. Gold streaks glisten in her hair under the autumn sun. Her cheeks blush and her skin glows, as radiant as if magic lived inside her. Perhaps humans have a magic of their own, or at least a few of them do... I feel my lips stretch in the faintest smile.

"I mean no harm to you, brother..." Vladimir says with a cautious tone. "But I don't think Father would have approved."

My stare cuts to him, imbued with a touch of fury. "Our father is not here," I mumble, vexed. How dare he bring Father into this?

Vlad clears his throat. His upper body shifts away from me. "He's not," he replies. "But the clan is, and I wouldn't want you to suffer any grievances because of them."

"The last time I chose a shifter, she betrayed me with my clan's former Enforcer," I say through clenched teeth. Bella is dead, murdered by Grisha's own claws. But the beast lives, and he's somewhere, hiding.

"I will see that Grisha's betrayal does not go

unpunished," he adds, letting me know that he's kept track of my life after all.

"I don't need your help, Vlad," I mutter. Reminiscing on my Enforcer's betrayal only heats my blood. "I will find him, and when I do, I will mark the end of his days." A pause. "My business is my own."

My brother's eyes narrow. He tilts his head, intrigued. "Is it?" Vlad asks. "You're the Ursa King now. Everyone expects you to make a match that will upraise the clan."

I sigh, reluctant to continue as I glimpse the end of this conversation. "You speak of the Deveraux witch…" I all but roll my eyes back.

Vlad steps closer. "Yes."

I am aware of the most powerful family of witches. My advisors have endlessly insisted on the match. "The one who lives in Paris," I say. "Jeanette."

"No," he breathes, shocked. "No, I mean Cassandra Deveraux. *She's* the heiress, Gavriil. She lives in the US."

I slip my hands into my pants pockets, and my stare drifts to Luciana. She sits on the fountain's stone rim, dipping her hand in the crystalline water.

"Heiress or not, I've already chosen my mate."

"Have you, Gavriil?" he asks with intent.

"Volodya…" I mutter.

"Have you claimed her?" Vlad is merciless.

I swing my head towards him, uttering a low growl. "I've not," I confess.

"And why haven't you, then?" he asks, inching closer. True concern gleams in his grey eyes. He sheds from his role as leader of the pack and shifts into my older brother, the one I grew up with. The one who always looked after me. His hand lands on my shoulder. The empath in me senses his sincerity, his absolute worry. "The truth may be harsh, but you yourself cannot deny it."

I move away from him. "Is that all you have to say?" I ask, putting a good three feet of distance between us. "After nearly a decade since you left me?"

Vlad's countenance gains pallor. "Gavriil, I could not live forever under your shadow…" he breathes, pain hanging from each word.

"So you created a shadow of your own," I mumble, looking away.

"My pack is my family now," he says with earnest eyes. "You and I will always be brothers… That is why I'm here." He purses his lips, hesitant to speak more.

After a minute, he adds, "*Family and duty come first,* Gavriil."

The bear in me bristles. "Must you throw Father's words at me like this?" I snap, wounded.

"I say these things because I care for you," Vlad says, keeping his distance. "I will not interfere with your choices. However, I ask that you consider what we've spoken." He inclines his head. "Your Majesty."

One step back, and he disappears inside the house.

"Family and duty come first," I mumble as warmth gathers in my eyes while I stare at Luciana. She's heading towards me. The closer she gets, the more concern overwhelms her delicate features.

24

GAVRIIL

I meet Luciana near the terrace. She blushes with a slight sun tan. It brings out the light freckles on her cheeks and nose. "Is he gone?" she asks, folding her hand on mine.

I nod in silence.

"Good," she says, gliding under my arm. We stroll around the fountain with sluggish steps. "I don't trust him."

I flinch in disbelief. "He's my brother," I tell her in a soft tone. "We grew up together. You don't know him like I do."

"I don't need to," Luciana replies, adamant. We halt and she slips out of my hold, standing in front of me. "If he's your brother, then where has he been for the past seven years? Touring Europe?" Her eyes narrow.

A pained expression mars my face. "You judge him harshly," I mumble. My gaze turns vacant. Deeper worries whirl in my mind.

"What is it?" she asks, concerned, while inching closer. "What did he tell you just now?" Her voice becomes soft as a caress.

I heave a sigh. I drift away from her and glide on the stone bench. There's no sense in hiding all I am. I cannot pretend my world is anything if not fueled with cruelty. I'm going to be honest with Luciana. She deserves to know the truth.

"Vlad reminded me of my station as leader of the clan," I begin, gazing downwards. "He reminded me I have great responsibilities to consider..."

"It's about me," she says knowingly.

I barely hold her stare for a few seconds, then I nod.

She rushes to me. "Gavriil, you don't have to listen to him," Luciana crouches until our eyes level, cradling my face between her soft hands. "One minute, Vlad is out of your life, and the next he's back, telling you what to do?"

My bear bristles. "I take orders from no one," I snap.

"Good. Then prove it!" she challenges. "Is this about claiming me? Well, then do it!"

"I can't…" I mumble, looking away from her sweet hazel eyes.

"Why not, Gavriil?" she demands. "Why won't you brand me?"

I rise from the seat. She straightens with me. "Do you want me to?" I say, defiant. "Do you want to be dragged into a world of murder and constant wariness? Is that what you want?" I'm almost hissing. "Please understand, if I claim you, your life will never be the same as it will be chained to mine forever." I pause to catch my racing breath. "An entire coven of vampires is after our heads… and this is but a glimpse of what would follow."

I think of Bella. I think of Grisha taking advantage of her heart, and me, incapable of shielding her from his viciousness. But I can protect Luciana. I can push her away from my ruthless world.

Her eyes shudder in dismay. "That is not…" she utters, but I cut her off.

"Do you even realize what becoming my mate would entail?" I say, narrowing my eyes. "I am the Ursa King. *You* are a human. Never in a thousand years has an Ursa King mated with a human… A shifter, yes. A witch, most assuredly. That's the kind of match expected from me."

Luciana's face loses all color. Her eyes glimmer with forthcoming tears. "So, what you're really saying is," she breathes, "that you do not care for me."

"I do…" I manage.

"Just not enough to make *that* commitment…" Her voice drifts into a hushed whisper.

My heart breaks in silence. "That is not what I'm saying," I say, stepping closer.

She recoils from me instantly. "No, why would you?" she adds, hugging her arms. "I mean, we've only just met… I'd rather know now how you feel." She swallows hard.

"Luciana, it's not that simple—" I reach to hold her arm, but she pulls her shoulder away.

"It is." She blinks, and a tear rolls down her cheek. "I've heard enough." She bridles and turns away.

"Luciana…" I go after her, but she dashes down the hall. Her slighting me like this spurs my bear into rabid fury. How dare she leave in the middle of an argument?

"Luciana!" I call. She does not look back. By the time I reach the vestibule, she's already on the stairway.

"Do not walk away from me!" I growl.

She leans on the balustrade, glaring down at me with bloodshot eyes. "You can't order me around, *Your Majesty*," she says, spitting my title like the foulest words. "I'm not one of your shifter subjects!"

"Clearly!" I retort, without moving an inch. My voice echoes in the hall. "If you were, you'd know better than to cross me!" I stop, chest heaving, heart racing. *Fuck.* I should not have said that. But I certainly cannot cower before her now.

Luciana's face slackens. "Are you threatening me?" she asks, shocked.

"People bend to my will where I come from," I mumble, frustration streaming through my veins. "Why can't you simply do as I ask?"

With widened eyes, I see her march down the remaining steps that lead back to the hall. And she doesn't stop until she stands before me. "Listen to me, Gavriil," she begins in the lowest of voices. "We are going to that gala. I'm getting rid of those vampires and rescuing Marco. And once that's dealt with... I never want to see you again."

She shatters me with her tongue. I can't back down. I won't. "A hard task when you live across the street," I tell her, impassive as I hold her stare.

"Then I'll move!" she mutters, tears rimming her hazel eyes.

"Don't trouble yourself," I reply in a dispassionate tone. "The minute this is over with, I'm going back to Russia."

"Good!" She marches upstairs.

"Fine!" I scowl.

Luciana's thudding footsteps dash down the hallway and into the bedroom. As my fury slowly fades, my hands quiver with anxiety. Suddenly, she storms out of the room carrying her gym bag, and heads downstairs in a hurry.

"What are you doing?" I mumble, letting my guard down. I can't afford to fight her anymore.

She stops at the front door. "Isn't it obvious?" she says with gritting teeth. "I'm going home."

I move closer. "You can't do this," I tell her in a low voice, when what I ache to scream is, *Don't do this to me.*

Luciana shoots one eyebrow skyward. "Oh, can't I?" she says, slipping her gym bag's strap on her shoulder. Her cheeks and nose blush. Pain stiffens her expression, not anger. "Watch me."

I follow her to the door. "Luciana…" I glide my fingers through my hair. How can I stop her? "It's dangerous," I say, subdued.

She glares at me with watery eyes. "I'm sure you can spare one of your many guards to keep watch over me," she says, and then pulls the door open.

My lips part, but no sound comes through. In an instant, Luciana is out and slams the door behind her. Hurt and frustration tangle in my throat. Every muscle in my body strains. A storm brews inside me, and when my body no longer can contain it, it comes out in a roar of grief.

I sweep every vase and picture frame from the credenza beside me. Porcelain and crystal shatter as they hit the floor. My balance falters and I lean against the wall. But as my anger wanes, it breaks me, and I slip to the ground. Tears of bitterness rim my eyes.

Did I not want her away from my life, where she could be safe? No. That's what my mind wanted, but my heart at all times whispered *no*... Why can't I change the hand fate has given me? Why must I always be this flawless figure of unrelenting power?

Father made it seem so easy.

I'm trying to do what's best for Luciana, what's best for my clan... Then why does it wound me so? I bury my face in my hands, painfully aware that by protecting her, I've destroyed the woman I love.

25

GAVRIIL

ours pass. I stay up all night, sitting by the window that faces her apartment. Like a fool, I hope she might look my way, peering through the pulled curtains. She does not. I can't even see if she's turned the lights on. My brother Dima keeps watch of her place. I sent him, along with four more members of the Elite, but Luciana refused to be protected by that many guards.

She will be safe under Dima's watch. I should be at ease. However, I can't stop staring at her window.

How long have I been awake? I don't know. Thunder rumbles outside, and a cool breeze filters through the windows. The skies are dismal. I cannot tell whether it's early in the morning or late in the evening.

It was an overcast afternoon when I met Luciana. Effortlessly, my lips curl into half a smile as I look back on that day. How she struck me with her heavy bag, ruthless as she fought for her vampire date. I think of the glare she gave me when Natalya sprayed her face... Finding her in the living room, lovely in her oversized white t-shirt. I remember making love to her. The total release of being myself with her—not the Ursa King. Not the Alexeev warlock. Just me. Gavriil.

Family and duty come first. I've stuck to my duty as my father always taught me, as Vlad so callously reminded me... Then why do I feel so rotten? Why do I feel like I've destroyed my one shot at happiness in life?

Fuck, this is messed up. *I* am messed up.

"Gavriil..." a soft voice says.

My gaze angles lazily to the bedroom's doorway, and I see my cousin standing there. Long chestnut hair and bangs framing her angelic face. She seems cozy, in dark denim and a cream wool turtleneck sweater. On top, she wears a brown leather jacket, sprinkled with water droplets.

Natalya moves closer. She sits next to me, on the floor. "дорогой..." *Sweetheart,* she calls me in my mother tongue. Her tender hand cups the side of my face.

My stare becomes vacant and strays to the floor. "What are you doing here?" I speak in Russian.

"Sasha called me," she says. A sigh escapes her lips. "He told me what happened."

I knit my eyebrows. "Did he?" I say, unsure of how I feel about my Enforcer's meddling.

Natalya flinches at the tone of my voice. She purses her lips. "He told me you've not slept or eaten since yesterday," she continues, folding her warm hand on mine. "He's worried." She exhales a long breath. "I am too." Her gaze glides to the window. "And this weather… It hasn't stopped raining since yesterday. I'm assuming you're behind it?"

"Possibly," I mumble, avoiding her stare. "What more did Sasha tell you?"

"That Volodya found you," she says, her voice drifting into a hushed whisper.

"He did." My manner is curt. Old fears and uncertainties rise with my brother's name. I cannot care less about the subject now.

"Gavriil…" Natalya says, leaning towards me.

Finally, I lock eyes with my cousin. "Can you see her?" I ask eagerly. "Can you make sure she's doing well?" Now I'm the one holding her hands. "If she needs anything…"

"If that is what you want, then I will see her," Natalya says, and her tone is imbued with genuine sweetness. "I care for her too. Do you know that?" Her dreamy eyes narrow as she nods.

I silently agree.

My cousin straightens, ready to rise when I seize her wrist. "Natalya," I breathe.

Her head swings towards me. "Yes?"

"Yours is the gift of sight," I begin. "I need to know… Have you seen our future? Do you see one for us?" My pulse skyrockets in an instant. Now that I've asked, I'm in full dread of the answer.

Natalya levels her stare with mine. "I see limitless love for each of you," she says with firm conviction. "Promise me you'll fix this."

"I will," I tell her, quickly waving aside any hesitation.

"Good." She rises and saunters to the doorway, where Sasha waits. They exchange silent words until Natalya leaves the room. Sasha does not.

My Enforcer steps inside. He drops a golden envelope on the night table. "For the gala," he says, sitting on the foot of the bed, facing me.

The storm subsides. Sasha clasps his hands

between his knees and looks out the window. "That's a start," he says, pleased. "Natalya's magic is absolutely impressive." He smiles.

"Are you seeing each other again?" I ask in a dull tone, longing to escape my tormenting thoughts.

"We are," Sasha says. It takes me by surprise for a second. But then, he adds, "As friends."

I frown, immediately drawn to sweep Sasha's expression. No pain contorts his face. No sorrow like the one I suffer. "Sasha, you and Natalya are meant for each other. How can you…?"

My Enforcer leans forward. "I will always love her, Gavriil," he's quick to say. "It's because I love her that I cannot force her back into my life." He bites his lower lip. "She's happy here."

I smooth a hand over my chin. "And what if it were the other way around?" I ask pensively.

"How?" Sasha says.

"What if she *wanted* to be part of your life?" I add.

My friend considers the question for a moment. The corner of his lips twists up. "Then I would be the happiest man in the world, Gavriil," he says. "But this is not about Natalya and me, is it?"

"It's not," I mumble. Uneasiness washes over me immediately. "Volodya, he said…"

"Vladimir left the minute you became king." Sasha frowns in disapproval. He interlaces his fingers. "I'm sorry, Gavriil, but it's true. His loyalty might be great indeed. His gratitude to the clan, unbroken, for taking him in when he became an orphan. But in the end, Vlad walked out when you needed him the most..."

"I love her," I breathe. The words come as a release from my misery. My heart quickens as I speak them loudly for the first time.

"Then all else shouldn't matter." Sasha rises from the bed and moves towards me.

"I am the Ursa King... She's human," I say, pain clenching my throat. "I should claim the Deveraux witch... I should..."

"You are the Ursa King," he says, pressing my shoulder. Sasha then crouches until his ice-blue eyes meet mine. "Good kings follow the rules... *Great kings rise above them.*"

His revelation strikes me full force.

"Life is too short to fill our days with senseless regrets. You can either choose a mate branded in duty, or choose one branded in love... The clan will support you, Gavriil," my Enforcer adds in reassurance. "*Always.*"

I gasp in relief. And my breathing picks up, harsh

and broken, as if I've emerged from freezing waters after being under for a very long time.

"I behaved badly towards her…" I mumble, ashamed.

Sasha smirks, raising his brow. "I'm sure she'll make you pay for it." He chokes a laugh.

"She will, won't she?" I smile bitterly. "If she'll have me, that is."

My Enforcer straightens. "I think you should find out," he says.

I get on my feet. "Yeah…"

"Just maybe have something to eat first, catch up on your sleep…" Sasha pauses. "And *please*, take a shower," he teases, a sly grin curling his lips.

26

LUCIANA

I turn off the television. The pitter-patter of rain fills the room in an instant. It's been like this for the past couple of days. I don't even want to pull open the drapes. The dreary weather will only deepen my wounds.

It's sweats and ice cream for me. I wasn't even ashamed yesterday when Natalya appeared at my doorstep. The poor woman. She looked at me as if I were a mess. And I am.

I used to be perfectly happy before I learned I was dating a vampire. I used to be wrapped in a boring ordinary life, but at least I didn't experience this much pain, this fathomless heartache. How the hell was I supposed to know I would fall so hard for Gavriil?

How did it even get to this point where I practically begged him to claim me?

And he refused.

I shut my eyes close. This has clearly been a one-sided affair from the beginning. And poor Marco, abducted by vampires… God, I feel so rotten. I need to get out of this place. I need to run, even if it's raining. That burly guy is standing in the hallway, but I don't care. I just need some fresh air to free myself from these horrible thoughts that haunt my mind, spinning in circles.

On an impulse, I grab my keys and rush to the door. I swing it open when suddenly, I see him, standing in the hallway. My breathing hitches. I freeze, eyes wide, trying to understand.

"Gavriil…" I barely speak.

He stares at me in silence, subdued like a wounded creature. "I'm sorry," he says in a low, soothing voice. The minute my lungs grasp the first whiff of his cologne, I'm drawn to him without remedy. I press a hand on the jamb, anchoring myself to the threshold.

"I've been a fool and an arrogant beast…" he begins.

A knot builds in my throat. I swallow hard. "You have," I say.

"I never should have listened to my brother."

"He was right, though," I tell him, heart pounding hard in my chest. "You're the Ursa King. I'm human and… we've only just met."

Gavriil steps close until we share the same breathing space. "Luciana," he breathes, "I don't need time to sort out my feelings. I know how I feel." He pauses. "I'm not here to play games. I am here, hoping you might look past my flaws."

"Gavriil, you don't have to—"

"I don't *have* to be here, and I am…" he says, and the corner of his lips curls as he echoes the words that once crossed my lips. "I don't *have* to love you, yet I do." His steady gaze bores into me in silent expectation. "I love you, Luciana."

My lips part, but no sound comes through.

"I know we can figure this out," he assures me, darkened eyes locked in mine. I do not refuse him as he holds my hands. "If you…" His voice breaks. "If you can find it in your heart to forgive me. To love me, after all I…"

"Shut up," I tell him, tears rimming my eyes. "I love you, Gavriil. I want to be with you… I want to see where this goes."

In a flash, he takes the last step that delivers him into my arms. His mouth finds mine in a desperate kiss, full of passion and longing. I cradle his face between my hands and step back into the house, pulling him with me.

He slams the door close with a kick of his heel and carries me effortlessly in his arms. I kiss his cheek, his neck. My hands explore his chest and tug at his clothes, aching for that nearness, that contact flesh on flesh.

We strip our clothes fast as we make it to the bedroom. I gasp as his bare body lies on top of mine, eager for the touch of his skin. I want him now. He reads my haste and skips all foreplay. His firm hands seize my hips and lift me to him, tucking my curves into his own.

My pulse skyrockets when a tormented groan sails through his lips. He then whispers, "Lie on your belly for me." He flips me over, spreading me beneath him. Gavriil grabs a fistful of my hair, tugging firmly as he lowers over me.

"Are you gonna…?" I manage, but the words break off in excitement.

"Only if you want me to," he purrs in my ear, making my entire body shiver in delight.

His searing lips nibble my earlobe, then glide down my neck, trailing passionate kisses. "I want you to claim me," I breathe. "Will it hurt?"

"Briefly," he says in a rough, husky voice. "We don't have to do this now, my love." A kiss on my nape. "I can wait until you're ready for me." A lick on my shoulder.

I writhe beneath him, imprisoned by his body in a web of arousal. "Do it," I beg with a low moan. "I want you, Gavriil. *All* of you." I long to become full of him.

A low growl lingers in his chest. His hardness slips between my thighs and slowly he sheathes himself inside of me. I moan in sweet ecstasy, elated, relieved.

He matches my lustful demands, making me soar high until I reach the brim of ecstasy. "Oh God…" I moan. "Don't stop." Waves of fathomless pleasure crash into my core and spread to my limbs. When I explode, I bring him with me. Gavriil's taut body convulses over mine. In a flash, he pulls my hair aside. His panting breath warms my shoulder. I sense the edge of his fangs as they graze my skin.

"Yes," I breathe, blissful tears prickling beneath my eyelids. "Do it."

A flash of lightning cuts through my flesh. The fangs, sharp stylets of merciless fury. I cry out in delirium, overtaken by tangled emotions. Fathomless pleasure and pain. It reminds me of my first tattoo; the heightened feeling of bliss, the merciless hurt that I welcome so willingly.

"Mine…" Gavriil moans against my shoulder. "Mine," he growls again, tightening his grip around my arms.

When his body clashes hard against me, his temple brushes the side of my face. And I listen to his panting breath, the words that linger in his throat, saying, "Gods… Oh gods…"

His firm hands glide under me. He rolls me over him as he lies on the bed, chest heaving, a swathe of perspiration glistening on his chiseled body. "Gods, I love you…" he says between quick breaths. He cradles my face in his hands. "I love you, Luciana."

My mouth finds his in one slow, heartfelt kiss. I then rest my head against his chest, listening to his quickened heartbeat as sweet exhaustion takes over us and wraps us in a pleasant dream.

Natalya

27

GAVRIIL

The purest bliss streams in my blood when I wake the next morning. I stare at her while she sleeps. My bite on her shoulder is but a slight bruise by now, healed quickly by my magic. A thrill rushes through me. For the first time in years, I've opened myself to love again. This time, it feels stronger and more real than it's ever been.

But restlessness finds a way into my joy. Tonight, we will face Andrea Barone and the members of his coven. Now, more than ever, I would not have Luciana expose herself to the dangers of these blood fiends. But I know well my say in it won't matter to her. And I know, too, that the only way for us to become free from their fangs is by destroying them.

I will take Andrea's head myself. I will avenge the reckless murder of my brothers. And I will stop the coven's vampires from getting anywhere near Luciana.

I rise from the bed and get dressed.

Meandering through Luciana's home, I text Sasha, instructing him to send over a gown, jewelry, and a stylist for her. He texts back with a thumbs-up emoticon and a winking face. I roll my eyes back. He's such a child. "And this is the man I chose as my Enforcer…" I say under my breath, going through the kitchen cabinets to make some coffee.

There is absolutely nothing in the pantry. The refrigerator is practically empty, save for a bottle of wine. *"Ой…"* I raise my brow in astonishment. No food whatsoever.

Finally, in a bottom drawer, I find instant coffee and a couple of sugar packets. "This will not do." I move to the entrance. My brother Dima might pick up a couple of espressos and maybe some flowers, too.

I open the door to find another man standing in the doorway.

"Vlad?" I mumble, unable to stop myself from frowning.

My brother's eyes widen slightly. I cannot tell whether he's surprised or simply glad to see me.

"Sasha told me where I could find you," he begins, combing back his ashen blonde hair with his fingers.

I step into the hallway and close the door behind me fast. "What is it?" I ask. "Is there a problem with our plan?"

"Quite the contrary," he says, slipping his hands into his jeans pockets. "I came to tell you that I've received confirmation. Andrea will be there tonight." He pauses, his stare drifting to the door behind me.

It bothers me that his interest seems to sway in that direction. I step aside and my body blocks the entrance completely. Vladimir might well be my brother, but at this point, I do not sense him that way. The bear in me bristles. *Do not cross this line, brother.*

"You could have called," I say, softening my harshness with, "and spared yourself the journey."

A faint smirk tugs at the corner of his lips. Vlad jerks his head back, raising his chin slightly. "We've been apart for so long," he says. "I thought I might tempt you with some coffee." He pauses. "Honestly, I didn't think I'd find you here." He smooths a hand across his chin, narrowing his grey eyes.

"Oh?" I say, crossing my arms over my chest. "And why is that?"

"Well," he breathes. "After our last conversation, I thought you might have… reconsidered."

A faint growl rests in my chest. Why is he here? I lean my body forward, feeling my expression tense with every inch as I get closer to his face. "She's mine, Vlad," I tell him in a hoarse whisper. "I've claimed her."

Vladimir's face slackens. "Oh…" he utters, stepping back. "Well, in that case… we might get that coffee some other time."

I nod slowly. "Some other time," I manage, struggling not to mutter the words. I don't like seeing him here. *Walk away,* I tell him with a fierce stare. *Don't ever let me find you here again, brother.*

He gets the message and takes one more step back.

"After we've ended Barone's coven," he adds with a wink.

"Yes," I reply, unfolding my arms. "That sounds good."

"I'll call you when it's done, brother." He casually turns and starts walking down the hallway. "We must celebrate as soon as possible!"

I say nothing, but my hard stare follows him until he disappears inside the elevator.

With the adrenalin still pumping in my veins, I start as the door creaks open behind me.

"Gavriil?" she says with a groggy voice, gorgeous in grey sweats and a messy hair bun.

Alertness gives way to relaxed bliss when my gaze meets her hazel eyes. My hand smooths over the side of her face, and a smile immediately blooms on my lips. *"Buongiorno, bellisima…"* I whisper, then press my lips to hers in a tender kiss. "How are you feeling?" I look at her shoulder.

She stares at it too. "Just a little sore," she says, surprised. "I thought it would be worse than this." Luciana's gaze glides to mine. "Are you…" she purses her lips, "leaving?"

"No," I hurry to say. "No, I'm not leaving." My hand folds over hers and presses it lightly. "Do you want some coffee?"

"I…" She looks back at the kitchen. "I think I might have some…"

"I mean outside," I add. "Do you want to grab some coffee and maybe walk in the park for a little while?"

Her face brightens with joy. "That sounds pretty good," she says, delighted.

"Great." I nod, returning her smile. "Let's go."

As we move down the hallway, I can't stop myself from soaring, for even on the brink of war between my clan and a coven of vampires, I have her. It's no longer *I*, but *we*. And that makes everything infinitely worth it.

*E*vening sets on the Roman horizon. Blood-red skies streaked with blue spread before the darkened city outline. We stand by the balustrade, champagne glasses in our hands. Warmth lingers in the air from the heaters that surround us. A quartet plays in the distance.

My gaze drifts away from the panoramic and lazily roves over Luciana, radiant in a sleeveless red chiffon dress with a plunging V-neckline. Her undiluted scent still drives me wild with lust, but the feeling is easier to tame now that I've branded her. I inch close to her. "You look so beautiful... I could have you right now," I whisper in her ear.

Her cheeks burn red scarlet. She bites her lower lip. I read her restlessness, understanding she's worried for her friend's sake, worried that the evening might shift from a precious fantasy into a true nightmare.

"Do you realize this is our first date?" I tell her, hoping to soothe her uneasiness.

She holds my hand, and hers quivers. "It would have been perfect had no vampires been involved."

I sweep a hand around her back, luring her close to me. She yields. "*You* are perfect…" I press my lips against her temple. "And it's going to be all right, my love," I assure her, even though the highest wariness spikes in my blood. "I'm taking care of this. Just stay close to me at all times."

She nods.

The guests gather near the central stage, where the chairman of the Arts Society pronounces some words of appreciation for our generous donations. We listen from a distance.

As the evening progresses, the number of people diminishes. A low bank of fog sifts through the woods and spreads to the terrace, muting the lamppost's lighting into a pale amber gleam. Out of the tree-lined pathway, I see the vampire emerge from the fog, like the preternatural demon that he is.

Andrea is not alone. Two vampires walk behind him. In an instant, the unveiled scent of Luciana's blood reaches the demon's nostrils and his fiery green eyes fix on us.

My senses pick up as Luciana's heart jolts into a gallop. My gaze remains locked on the vampire, but my hand glides around her arm.

"It's him, isn't it?" she whispers.

I nod in silence.

Andrea halts before reaching the terrace. He would not dream of confronting a shifter in a crowd of mortals. Secrecy is vital for a vampire, as essential to their survival as their obsession for human blood.

A smirk tugs at the vampire's lips.

I take the champagne saucer off Luciana's hands and set both on the stone balustrade. Then, holding her hand, we stroll across the terrace.

"Gavriil…" she whispers in a wary tone. "We're going straight to them?"

"Yes," I answer in a low, dispassionate tone.

"Oh, fuck…" she says under her breath.

I stare at her, dumbfounded.

"What?" she says, unnerved.

"I don't think I've ever heard you curse before, is all." I shrug.

"Well, get used to it." She bites her lower lip. "Especially if this kind of thing becomes my new normal."

"It won't," I say in reassurance.

She releases a long, broken breath.

"Let me do the talking," I tell her as we stand a few feet from meeting the vampire trio. I'm sure there's more, hiding in the shadows, as blood drinkers usually do.

Andrea raises his chin slightly to meet my eyes. An insufferable smirk tenses his lips. He thinks he's better than everybody, especially better than a shifter. *Animals,* they call us. *Beasts.*

"Gavriil Alexeev," he begins. "The Ursa King himself. Here, in my city."

"I didn't realize you owned Rome," I reply.

He utters a short laugh and looks at his friends. "Well, maybe not all of it." He shrugs his shoulders. "But a great deal of the city, yes."

I look down at Andrea and give him half a smile.

Rub it in, demon. This is your hunting ground, not mine. But that won't stop me from tearing your head off.

Behind me, the lights dim. The gala is over. Only vampires and shifters remain, and one very special human.

"How should we do this, Gavriil?" Andrea asks with aloofness.

"That depends," I say, scratching an eyebrow. "I

would appreciate sparing myself the effort of killing you."

The vampire chokes a laugh. "You amuse me," he says. "I'm taking the human, Gavriil," he says. "I suggest we do this peacefully. As you might suspect, I am not alone tonight."

In a flash, the blood in my veins burns like liquid lava. Every muscle in my body goes taut with alertness. My breathing quickens. Sasha waits for my signal.

"I know you killed my son," Andrea says through clenched teeth, fury contorting his expression. "I'm willing to let that go… in exchange for the woman." He pauses. "If I were you, I'd take my generous offer. She's just a human, after all."

LUCIANA

Gavriil's grip tightens. His hand glides away from mine instants before his hold becomes painful. A growl rumbles in his chest. His dark brown eyes turn black as he leans forward.

"I do not appreciate how you addressed my girlfriend," he says in a hoarse voice. "Apologize. Right. Now." His nostrils flare, his chest heaves.

"Your *girlfriend?*" Andrea mocks.

"Is that what shifters call their bitches nowadays?" says the vampire to Andrea's right.

In a flash, Gavriil's hand seizes the blood drinker's throat. I see human hands change under the play of light and shadows. Hair covers flesh, claws break beneath his fingernails. The vampire's neck cracks when his grip clenches. Then his eyes roll blank and the blood drinker drops to the ground.

The vampire to Andrea's left screeches in response, but leaps back instead of forward.

I can't breathe. My mouth dries in an instant.

"You're… next," Gavriil roars, pointing at the head vampire.

As my gaze sweeps over the copse, I see shifters dropping from the treetops. Vampires materialize out of nowhere and both clash in a whirlwind of growls and hissing.

"Get her!" Andrea points at me with a crooked finger.

I gasp in dread. I should have brought a gun, a knife, *anything* to fight back—not that it would have made much of a difference.

The second vampire lunges towards me, quick as lightning. In a blink, he stands inches away from me, baring fangs, claws ready to seize me. With the same unnatural speed, Gavriil appears out of the corner of my eye. He stands under a tree, tears off a branch and breaks it on his knee, then throws the pointy end at the vampire, and like a spear, it breaks through the blood drinker's chest. Blood spatter bursts from the wound with full force, staining my dress with a few droplets.

I take my quivering hand to my lips and jump back.

"Luciana," someone hisses in my ear.

I look back, overwhelmed and shuddering. Relief washes over me when my gaze meets ice-blue eyes.

"Sasha!"

"Come with me!" he says, holding my arm. "I'm getting you out of here!"

I turn to Gavriil, chasing after Andrea down the avenue while dodging vampires, brawling and fighting werebears.

"Luciana!" Sasha tugs at my arm harshly, dragging my focus away.

"But, Gavriil…!"

"He'll be fine!" he assures me. "Let's go!"

GAVRIIL

I chase the fucking monster down the lane, but he vanishes in an instant. Furious and frustrated, I stop at the fountain. Nothing but trees surround me. My senses are keen enough to pick up the faintest noise, but Andrea is stealthy. His scent, however, permeates the air.

"Your foul stench betrays you, Andrea…" I growl. Putrid human blood, centuries old, sticking to his gums. "Let's end this now."

I narrow my gaze, sweeping through the mass of trees. He won't dare to appear on the gravel road. Slowly, I remove my suit's jacket, revealing the harness where I strapped my throwing axe. I drop the jacket on the fountain's stone rim and roll my sleeves up to my elbows.

"I could kill you with my bare hands, vampire…" I continue, holding my axe in a firm grip. "But where's the fun in that?"

I follow the scent, away from the road and into the woods. *This* is my arena. "I killed your son, Andrea. He wasn't fast enough…" I taunt him. "You sired a lousy vamp. Do you hear me?"

Dried twigs crack behind me.

"You're an arrogant motherfucker," I mumble as my lips stretch in a knowing smile.

The scent shifts from my back to at least ten feet in front of me. Narrowing my gaze, I make out the creature's silhouette. I turn away from it, but hold it with a side glance.

Come and get me.

"Do you know why there are no vampires left in Saint Petersburg?" I say.

A gust of wind rushes towards me from the side. Fast as lightning, I twist my torso and swing my axe in silver fury. The vampire materializes in the middle of the forest, blade buried deep in his chest.

Andrea drops to the ground. I trudge to him before the creature has a chance to heal.

Towering over the vampire, I pull the axe away, watching the red ruin that drenches his tailored white shirt. I tilt my head, glaring at him with an icy stare, and wait for his wild eyes to latch on mine.

"It's because I never miss," I tell him. My axe swings down, chopping off the demon's head in a single blow.

LUCIANA

Panic riots in my heart as I wait near the parking lot. It's been quiet for a while now. The silence is deafening and makes my mind flutter away in sheer anxiety. A cold knot clenches my stomach. I clasp my hands, unable to part my eyes from the treelined edge of the park.

All tension flees from me the minute I see Gavriil emerge from the fog-veiled woods. Tall and hulking, he marches down the avenue, alone.

"Gavriil…" I manage, moving to meet him.

"Luciana!" Sasha grabs my arm and pulls me back. "Wait!"

My head swings back to him, perplexed. Why does he stop me? "It's him!" I tell him, struggling to break free from Sasha's firm hold. It's useless. "It's him! Let me go!"

"Not until I know it's *really* him," Sasha urges, hauling me behind him.

I glare at him in dazed exasperation. "What do you mean?" My furious gaze stabs his back.

Sasha straightens, every inch of him stiffened in alertness. He looks back over his shoulder. "It takes a while for the bear to leave after a fight," he says in reassurance. "It could be dangerous... *Please*. Let me make sure."

My feelings tangle in hope and fear. I nod.

"Wait here," he says between quick breaths. Sasha's expression hardens when he moves towards Gavriil.

As Gavriil trudges closer, I notice his white disheveled shirt, drenched in blood. He wears a brown leather harness strapped around his shoulder, where he carries a modest throwing axe.

Within minutes, Sasha and Gavriil stand face to face. Sasha talks to him in a gentle tone. I can't hear the words. He presses a hand on Gavriil's chest, making him stop. This does not sit well with him. Gavriil sneers and shoves Sasha away, thrusting his shoulder back with his hand.

Gavriil keeps walking. Sasha stops him again.

They argue. But Sasha is adamant and doesn't stop until Gavriil does. Then his gaze drifts downwards, and slumping his shoulders, Gavriil shakes his head. He sweeps a hand across his eyes, his expression a grimace of pain and weariness. Sasha takes a hand to his shoulder. Gavriil wraps him with his arm and pulls him close in a heartfelt embrace.

When they part, Gavriil and Sasha walk together towards the parking lot.

Gavriil stops a few feet away from me, avoiding my stare. The silence between us is long and brittle. His eyes meet mine for a second, and I recognize immense grief in them. I don't know how many of his brothers fell tonight, but I know a single one would be too many.

"The car's waiting," Sasha says with no inclination. He takes the lead. We follow him, trudging all the way.

Gavriil's tension slowly thaws when we sit in the car. Sasha sits next to the driver. He closes the door. The vehicle starts to move.

Sasha's phone rings, and he answers with a quiet voice.

"Gavriil..." I begin, not knowing what to say. I swallow with difficulty and force myself to speak. "Did we win?" My gaze glides to his black bespoke trousers, smeared with dirt and dark blotches of dried blood.

His firm hand smooths on my knee. "We *won*..." he says with an empty stare. Bitterness clings to each word.

My hand folds on his. Then, gently, I pull it towards me and press it against my lips.

Gavriil startles, becoming instantly awake. His gaze finds mine, darkened brown eyes full of sorrow. His hand glides away from my hold and cups the side of my face. "I'm sorry you had to see that..." he whispers, pain straining his expression.

Tears rim my eyes. "I only care that you're alive," I say in a broken voice. A tear rolls down my cheek. He smears it away with a soft stroke of his thumb. A wry smile thins his lips. In an instant, he pulls me to him, trapping me in his powerful arms corded in muscle.

"We have him," Sasha says, tilting his head towards us. "Marco." He pauses. "They're taking him to the house."

My breath catches in my throat as my heart sprints into a gallop. "Is he okay?" I beg, despair breaking through me.

"He's alive," Sasha tells me. He then turns away and points out something to the driver.

He's alive. I cover my mouth with my hand, but it's too late. A quiet sob sails through my lips.

Dawn spreads on the horizon as the car drives down Via Flaminia. Gavriil holds me tight, and for that, I'm thankful. Every bone in my body feels as if it's turned into dust. I just want to go home.

3 2

LUCIANA

With haste, I pick up my gown's train and dash up the manor's front steps before Sasha and Gavriil reach the entrance. The doors are open. A wave of apprehension falls over me as I consider the state in which I'll find Marco. I will never forgive myself for the harm those vampires might have caused him. It's all my fault. I should have answered his phone calls, should have texted him back. But I was too busy holding childish anger and resentment against him... What good is it to think of it now? I push those thoughts to the back of my mind.

My heels clank against the marble checkerboard floor when I storm into the vast hall. A horde of men gather in the vestibule, members of Gavriil's Elite.

There are unfamiliar faces too, however. I'm guessing they're members of Vladimir's pack.

Dima is standing in the center of the hall. "Where is he?" I ask him in a soft voice.

His dark green eyes set on mine for an instant. Dima tilts his head towards the parlor. I nod and move past the group, each breath burning in my throat.

I open the parlor's doors, fearful of what I'll find. More men crowd the room, concealing the view from me. In an instant, I hear Marco's voice. He's finishing a story in his usual blasé tone. Roaring laughter rises from the Ursa men... Bemusement washes over me. I push my way through the horde. And finally, I see Marco—lounging on a sofa, sipping from a glass of whisky on the rocks.

Marco's mask of indolence fades the minute his eyes land on me. He puts the drink away and shoots to his feet.

"Marco..." I breathe, sweeping him with an appraising stare. It takes me a moment to realize he's unharmed. Or at least that's what it looks like.

Without saying a word, Marco races to my arms. He holds me and comforts me, when it should be the other way around. Tears stream down my cheeks, and I sob like a girl while I hold him even tighter. "Marco!" I gasp. "You're all right!" But what I really mean is, *You're alive.*

Marco parts from me, briefly, and looks into my eyes. "I'm all right, *cara*..." he assures me, smearing away the tears from my cheeks. "No bites or anything." He wraps an arm around my shoulders and takes me to the couch where we sit.

"Now, let me begin by saying..." He throws me a knowing look. "I told you I didn't like that Trent dude!" Marco scowls at me playfully.

A bitter smile twists my lips. I nod and sniff, more composed now. "Did they do anything to you?" I ask him in a shaky voice.

"Oh, I wish! They were *so* gorgeous," Marco says, looking at the gathering of Ursa men. They laugh and heckle him for preferring vampires over shifters. "I'm joking, guys. Honestly!" He grins and faces me. "Turns out, my blood is not all that appealing to vampires." He shrugs in regret. "They were so obsessed with you, they never took an interest in me."

"God, Marco..." I shake my head. "That sounds horrible!" Despite his perpetual merriment, I'm sure it must have been terrifying.

Marco holds my hand with warmth. "The minions treated me like a guest," he adds in a more serious tone. "The vampire boss… not so much." Marco sneers.

"He's dead now," Gavriil says in a dispassionate voice.

I turn to the doorway and see him. Chestnut hair tied back into a low bun, cleaned up and wearing a fresh change of clothes. Casual jeans and a black pullover sweater.

Marco raises a groomed eyebrow. "Well, good riddance! That dude was nasty." He cracks a smile and relaxes on the couch. "So, you guys are really shifters," he adds, eyes widened in amazement. Marco glances at the horde. "Bears and wolves!"

Gavriil slips next to me. "I can take his memories away," he speaks close to my ear, a warm hand folded over mine. "You're his friend, my love. Would you want me to do it?"

"Don't you dare, Gavriil!" Marco gasps, aggrieved. "This is the most exciting thing that has happened to me in my entire life! Don't you *dare* take this away from me!" He frowns, vexed.

My gaze angles to meet Marco's. A smile quirks the corner of my lips. "I think he's gonna be all right," I say.

Gavriil's fingers interlace with mine.

Murmurs rise from the horde. They step back,

making way for someone. My head swings to the entrance where I see Vladimir standing at the doorway, back perfectly straightened and shoulders squared. Tall and imposing as Gavriil, his silver eyes glinting with magic. The hardness of his expression slowly fades into an easy smile.

"It's over," he says in a low, velvety voice.

"Brother..." Gavriil rises from the seat. He welcomes Vlad with open arms, embracing him fast. When they part briefly, Vladimir cups the side of Gavriil's face with fondness. Both of them smile.

"Thank you," Gavriil utters, gaze locked in Vlad's silver eyes.

The wolf's lips twist into a smirk. "Just like the old days," Vlad says, stepping back. "I will always be here for you, brother. I will always stand by you... no matter what you choose." His sharp stare drifts above Gavriil's shoulder and stabs me with intensity. I shiver immediately.

"Breakfast is ready," a familiar voice says.

All heads veer to the doorway.

Gavriil's face brightens with joy. "Natalya..." He goes to her and greets her at the entrance with a warm hug. "You came."

She nods in silence. "Congratulations, cousin." Natalya slowly parts from him, but holds his arms with fondness. "You did it. You've dismantled the Roman coven." She pauses, a swathe of nostalgia veiling her expression. "My uncle would be so proud..."

"Natalya," Vlad mumbles, sneaking out from behind Gavriil.

A glint of coldness shimmers in Natalya's eyes. "Volodya," she says, offering him her cheek. Vladimir kisses it while holding her hands.

Her gaze drifts across the room. A moment later, Natalya comes upon me. A flash of joy passes over her face. "Oh, *printsessa!*" she says, sauntering to join me.

I rise from the seat and go to her. Natalya's hugs are the absolute best in the world, and I need one badly. Warmth and love pour into my weary soul when she holds me. Her delicate fingers travel up my back, and stop on my right shoulder. I feel her smile. "You're one of us now, Luciana," she speaks in my ear. "Welcome to the family."

"What about me?" Marco says, getting on his feet. "I was kidnapped by vampires. That must account for something."

Natalya stares at Marco, eyes widened in bewilderment. Her luscious lips ease into a forgiving smile. "You can be part of our clan as well," she tells him.

"Now..." Natalya turns, glancing at the horde that crowds the room. "Let's eat. I bet everyone's starving!"

Wolf and bear shifters move out of the parlor; some wrapped in each other's arms, others sharing stories of the recent clash with the vampires. Sasha lingers by the doorway, waiting for Natalya. When she reaches him, they exchange quiet words and shy glances. Finally, Sasha's hand folds over hers and they walk into the hallway.

Vladimir follows them, but then Marco catches up with him at the door. He and Vlad talk on their way out. They haven't made it to the corridor when Marco starts asking him shifter-related questions.

Now the room is empty, except for Gavriil and me. We stand facing each other in silence. Him, comfortable in cozy autumn clothes. Me, wearing last night's lavish red gown.

"You're gonna love it here," he says, boring his maroon eyes into mine.

"I already do," I tell him, gliding my hand over his.

His gaze drops to the floor. "I bet those heels are killing you right now," he adds with a hint of mischief.

I look up at him in amused wonder. "They really are," I blurt.

In a flash, Gavriil pulls me to him. I shriek, fully surprised, as he sweeps me off the ground and gathers me to his arms. "Let's go," he purrs.

I laugh and wrap my arms around his neck, then nestle against his chest. In his arms, I am whole and happy. And as we cross that threshold, I know this bliss is but a glimpse of our happiness for many years to come.

ABOUT THE AUTHOR

Silvana G. Sánchez is the USA TODAY bestselling author of sinfully addictive dark fantasy new adult novels *Ash and Snow, Steel and Stone, Written in Blood,* and more paranormal and fantasy romance stories, including the *Vesely Academy* series. She lives in Mexico with her husband, son, and two adorable Shih-Tzus she calls her dragons. When not plotting away in her writing den, she's known to poke eyes in her practice as an ophthalmologist.

For more information:
silvanagsanchez.com
sgs.author@gmail.com

www.ingramcontent.com/pod-product-compliance
Lightning Source LLC
Chambersburg PA
CBHW030823210726

48290CB00002B/725